I0752890

# Black Hollywood

## The New Atlanta

# Black Hollywood

## The New Atlanta

Bennie Thomas

Published by:
Three C Publishing
880 Glenwood Ave SE
Suite#3559
Atlanta, Georgia 30316

In conjunction with:
Old Mountain Press, Inc.
85 John Allman Ln.
Sylva, NC 28779

www.oldmp.com
Old Mountain Press eBook Division
www.oldmp.com/e-book
910-476-2542



Interior text design by Tom Davis
Cover design by Jason Sketcher X Collins
**ISBN:** 979-8-9875809-4-3

Black Hollywood: The New Atlanta


First Edition
Printed and bound in the United States of America by Morris Publishing®
3212 East Highway 30
Kearney, NE 68847
1-800-650-7888
www.MorrisPublishing.com
10 9 8 7 6 5 4 3 2 1

# PROLOGUE..

WHILE GROWING UP in the hood, the narrative that I was led to believe was that this place called America was the land of the free. From my perspective it didn't feel like anything was free to me. However I had a true hustler for a father and he showed me how to bend some of the rules of the game and get some *Freebandz* as I like to call them from the land. In my opinion I felt like I had been taught by the best, and that was "*Frank White*!'. In the streets he went by '*White*' Back In the days I saw a lot of dudes hustling, and getting money but when it came to White and hustling, those two went together like Atlanta and Hollywood, which both were all about the come up.

*White* had the east side streets of Atlanta on lock, and that was big facts! But *White* had one problem that he just couldn't shake. And that was how *White* loved living the flashy and luxurious lifestyle. At the age of 12, I had the opportunity to move into an upper middle class neighborhood where our neighborhoods average household earning income was over six figures. The community was also more kid friendly and the police didn't have to sit on every corner.

The house that my father *White* bought us sat in the middle of *Clairmont Road* in the suburbs, where the price ranges of the homes started at a quarter of a million dollars. The house we owned in Kirkwood was also nice. However, it was no comparison to our three story, four bedroom, five bathroom home on Clairmont. We had a pool, tennis court, exercise room and a full length basketball court with the initials 'Z6 ' in the middle of the court. 'Z6 'stood for 'Zone 6 'which was the neighborhood that we were originally from before we got to Clairmont Rd.

The four car garage attached to the house held Frank's black Porsche 911 with peanut butter colored interior along with two old school Chevrolets. When the family would partake in events like Ben Hill day, Edgewood day, East Lake day, Birthday Bash, or any other Hood affair we would bring out one of his two Chevrolet Donk's. One of them was my favorite, it was the 1969 Chevrolet Impala. It had a chrome grill, a chrome blower that came out of the hood, and a pair of twenty two inch butnic's rims on the front. On the back of the ride was a pair of twenty one inch rims that sat staggered from the front.

The paint job that the custom paint shop named Godfather's Customs laid on the Chevrolet was showroom floor material. It was pearl white, and when the sun shone on the paint job it faded to a reddish orange. The interior was soft white with a red stitching that lined the seats. The other Chevrolet was similar, except the color was different. This one had the same fade, but its dominant color was black.

MY MOM, *TINA WHITE* was a homebody. A job for her was never an option in White's eyes. My mom and father had been together ever since high school. If you knew Mrs White, one thing was definitely understood, and that was how outspoken she was in every situation. She never had a problem speaking her mind and I must say to have been living on this earth for 55 years, she didn't look not a day over 35. As her son I prided myself on how well she took good care of herself.

*Monique White*, my heart. My sister. But man, she's just too much for TV. I'm not sure if there's a dude walking the streets of Atlanta that can make her happy. Because of the way White spoiled her growing up, I just knew that the dude was going to have hell to pay for her genuine time and energy. But if there was someone that caught her eye, he definitely had to be on the same level as *White* or doing better than he was.

Then there's me. *Frank White Jr.* I never liked living under my father's name, so my family called me *J. R.* but in the streets I went by *Fernando.* My father *White* always said that I should be my own man. He always encouraged me to set examples for others and learn how to follow before I could lead.

My leadership qualities came from watching my father closely. I grew up and took notes on how he maneuvered and built his business from the ground up. On my 19th birthday, *White* bought me a Range Rover and a Porsche Cayenne. He had them delivered to our home on a flatbed tow truck. I was a happy young man to say the least.

Six months after my father *White* ushered me into my first stage of manhood, he was out with a friend driving down *Peachtree Street.* They had just left from a strip club called *Diamonds Of Atlanta.* He and his friend decided that they would stop by *Uptown* Comedy club on *Marietta Street.* When they were about half a mile away from the club white decided that he would allow a driver who was riding his bumper to pass him. *White* merged over slowly as the unidentified driver pulled alongside him so that he could pass. However, the driver did not pass *White* at all. Muzzle flashes and gunshots exit an automatic weapon as it aims and hits *White* 17 times.

*White* died instantly. Suspiciously, his friend was only grazed across the head and neck from the gunshots. That night was a tragedy for the *White* family. Three years later there still had been no traces or information about the whereabouts of the shooter or anything else pertaining to *Frank White's* death.

One thing I prided my dad on was preparing for the inevitable. White had a healthy fortune saved up for his family just in case of an unforeseen incident of that magnitude. We were devastated and that incident shook our family world. My sister *Monique* stayed at home with our mom *Tina*, however I had people to see and places to be. Plus the house that we lived in left too many memories of my father and that made it hard for me to continue to wake up every morning being surrounded by everything that white had built.

THE TOP FLOOR at the Cotton Mill lofts on Auburn Avenue made me fall in love at first sight. The loft was decorated with a cherry wood spiral staircase that led to the balcony of my master suite. Hardwood floors lined all of the other bedrooms in the loft and the warm colored walls allowed each painting to sit comfortably in its place. The master suite was beige in color. A 75 inch TV was mounted to the wall above a white marble table. The California King bed was set perfectly in its place with the 10,000 thread count sheets resting on the mattresses. The size of the walk-in closet in the master suite put an average bedroom square footage to shame. The shoe racks lined the walls and hailed Giuseppe Zanotti, Gucci, Prada, Louis Vuitton and damn near every pair of retro Jordans that was ever made.

Living in the luxury Cotton Mill lofts allowed me to rub shoulders and talk politics with most of Atlanta's hottest rappers and movers and shakers. I was able to shine and flex my muscles with the best of best. However, I learned that that is how my father *White* ended up getting clipped, he flexed his muscle a little too much. I had seen a few bad moves that he had made in the past so I decided for the most part that I would take in most of the good things that he taught me, however I still carried with me a few of his bad habits.

# CHAPTER I

## It Goes Down In The EA...

Today was one of those days that you just couldn't miss out on! It was Glenwood day! The traffic was backed up on Glenwood Rd, from Candler road, all the way up to Covington highway. This was a time for us to shine, and most of us did just that. The guys brought out their fast cars, designer clothes, and loud weed smoke. Because of that, the bad bitches were everywhere. Most of the girls wore their skimpiest clothing that they had in order to show off their goods.

That day was no different for Fernando, because he wanted to steal the show and pull out his 1965 Ford Mustang fastback. However, a call came in from the auto shop informing Fernando that his nitro tank hadn't arrived yet so he couldn't drive that particular vehicle. As a backup plan Fernando decided to drive his Range Rover but he never liked to half step so he decided that he would go to *Third World Automotives* so that they could replace his factory rims with a pair of all black 24-inch Forgiatos.

As he is driving, his dash board lights up letting him know that he has a incoming call.

"What it do, Deon?" Fernando said.

"Tell me something good fam?"Deon said.

"I'm over here trying to make it to Glenwood Day bro. What are you up to?" Fernado responded.

"You should have hit me up earlier bro. Hold on one second Deon."

Fernando says, as he merges over to the other side of the road.

"I'm back bra, I'm glad you called because me shit I just left Third World getting mounted up, so as soon as I get off the highway I'm headed your way!"

"I'm here my nigga." Deon said.

"Give me a few minutes. Hey Deon!" Fernando quickly added.

"I'm still here. What's up?" Deon quickly responded.

"I know you got some weed over there?"

"And you know it!" Deon boasted with excitement.

"I got this rapper weed shawty and this shit on another planet my nigga!" Deon said

"Stop spraying them folks like that! Rapper weed! I believe it when I see it bruh!" Fernando said sarcastically.

"I ain't flexing! This pack came straight from Cali. and the label says, California Moon Rock!" Deon says with confidence.

"Moon rock! Hold that thought bro!" Fernando said, and then hit the end button on the touch screen.

Fernando presses the gas trying to make it to Edgewood Court in a record time.

The Edgewood community had been revitalized up and down Mason Avenue because gentrification had begun. Most of the people who lived in the neighborhood moved over to Edgewood Court Apartments during the remodeling. Due to gentrification and its renovations, townhouses were also being built on Hosea Williams drive all the way back up to Mason Ave toward Candler Park train station, so when you turned off of Mason Avenue onto Hardee Street at the red store heading towards Edgewood Court apartments, the scenery drastically changed.

Fernando circled the parking lot until he found a spot to park. He stepped out of his ride and was met by a pretty young lady named *Nicole. Nicole* was the daughter of a hood boss named '*Nasty Red*' *White* and *Nasty* got money together and they even engaged in some politics when White was alive. There were rumors of *Nasty* having connections to the murder of *White*. But when investigators questioned *Nasty*, his alibi checked out and his witness showed up to testify on *Nasty Red's* behalf.

As *Nicole* grew older in age she began to become infatuated with the other hustler's, mainly because of *Nasty Red* raising her as a single father. That's all she saw, and on top of that there was nothing around the house but gangsters, hustlers and killers. In school she messed around with a few dudes, but being associated with *Nasty Red* there was very little that she could do without him knowing.

The day of *Nicole's* graduation came and went as if it never happened, and so did *Nasty*. *Nasty* wasn't present at the graduation because there was urgent business that needed to be handled on the west coast. The position *Nasty* held with his plug, didn't allow *Nasty* to have any excuses for not showing up. There were no exceptions. When he took off, so did *Nicole*. She decided to pack her bags with the mind frame of starting over with being in control of her own life.

*Nicole* had been spoiled and all she was accustomed to was, whatever she asks for, she got. Nicole stood 5'6, and weighed 135 lbs. She was the perfect height and weight with pretty black long hair. She had a medium cup size breast. She was a dark brown cute faced girl with a slim waist that curved over to her heart shaped ass. Her cute face and slim waist landed her a job at the strip club called **D.O.A.**

After 6 months on the job, she ran into this dude named *Rich Boy*. After three formal dates, several sexual encounters, it was no turning back from *Rich Boy* for *Nicole*. *Rich Boy* decided to cuff *Nicole* instantly, so he insisted that *Nicole* move into one of his apartments in Edgewood Court. *Rich Boy* was known for selling a little weed on the side which helped him maintain his habit, but his main hustle was moving guns. Whenever *Rich Boy* would travel throughout the black market handling his business, he made sure that he kept up with the latest outfits.

*Fernando* did business with *Rich Boy* because of his gun collection. Whenever *Fernando* would pull up, he noticed the look that *Nicole* always gave him when he and *Rich Boy* transacted their business. The look that *Nicole* gave *Fernando* always made him wonder if there was anything special between the two of them. That day was no different because before *Nicole* got into her car, he could have sworn that he heard her silently say to him," Imma call you"

Once *Fernando* reached *Deon's* place, he jumped out of his ride and made sure that he took his Glock 40 and put it in the back of his waistband before heading up to the apartment. *Deon's* residence was decorated with pictures of weed buds, *Bob Marley,* and of the Jamaican flag. *Deon* wasn't Jamaican, but he just loved getting high like the Jamcians. The furniture was dark colored with two 60 inch TVs hanging side by side in the living room that played the sports stations Espn and Espn2 on them.

"Let me check out this moon rock!"Fernando said as he picked up the pack and smelled the hybrid fragrance.

Fernando inhales the aroma of the weed and says, "Say fam who's selling this shit? I ain't never seen no shit like this before!"

"Old school from *Tony Valley on Candler Road*, but I'mma let you know beforehand that this might be the highest weed in the city right now." Deon said.

"So what was the ticket on the pack?" Fernando asked,

"Shiiit fitty a gram!" Deion responded

Fernando gave Deon a questionable look.

"I'm going to have to hit you up later, cuz if I cop two or better of them whole thangs, ain't no way shawty going to try me like that!" Fernando says with conviction.

Dion started breaking down the weed.

"Check this out, ain't no smoking this bud without mixing another strain of weed. See this **THC** right here? Deon pointed.

"THIS WHAT MAKES it hard to light in a blunt, but if we had a bong, we'll get high as fuck today!"

"How about we do that some other time. All we need right now is a few blunts rolled up, and us on the road. Cuz I know we are missing out on all the action." Fernando said.

"Word!" Deon responded as he kept rolling up the blunts.

CANDLER RD WAS busy that day, and traffic was backed up. Police were everywhere and the hood definitely came out to play. Fernando initially started to hit Glenwood from Memorial Dr. to Candler Rd. because of the traffic. Instead he kept straight up Memorial Dr. and turned onto Columbia Dr and drove East to Glenwood Rd through the back streets. Fernando pulled into the *Checkers* parking lot on Columbia and Glenwood after spotting a few of his homies from Kirkwood's Lil Mexico. They were parked side by side in several different foreign vehicles.

"That boy Nando!" *Scooter* shouted, with his right hand held up to his forehead, giving him a salute.

"Shawty you stay flexing!" *Scooter* continues with the accolades.

Fernando and Deon stepped out of his ride blowing on the good green that was in their hands. *Scooter* sat admiring the SUV and took notice of the way the forgiatos had Fernando's Range Rover sitting pretty.

"Yeah, y'all rich ass niggas the ones eating, while I'm barely getting by." Fernando said in a meek tone.

"Nigga please!" *Mexico Ran* said sarcastically with passion in his voice.

Everybody broke out laughing.

*Meathead* walks up with his nose in the air as he smells the weed and says, "Aye Nando, what the hell kind of gas is that! That shit stank bro!"

Fernando passes *Meathead* the blunt and says, "This some shit Deon had, it's called *Moon Rock!*"

"*Moon Rock*!" *Meathead* says.

"Yeah *Moon Rock*! You ain't heard about that *Moon Rock*! Man you slipping!" Deon says.

*Meathead* smells the aroma from the blunt before inhaling it, and everybody gathers around and waits for their turn to hit the newest weed that was on the block. Deon and Fernando looked at each other at the same time as the crew rushed the scene and waited for the chance to experience the New *Moon Rock* weed.

As everyone is waiting to hit the weed a red Bentley GT Continental pulls up bumping a song by The Migos. It was *Rudy,* One of *Lil Mexico's* finest and one thing for sure is every time *Rudy* came around something was definitely about to go down. *Rudy* was one of the most well-known street niggas in "The A"

On top of having street cred he also did his thing in the rap game. The Migos track blast through the Bentlerys *Naim* sound system "Look at my dab/err body saying dab"

Instantly the whole crowd turned their heads. The sight of the red Bentley GT Continental pulling up in the hood was an inspiration for everyone in *Lil Mexico.*

"Look at my dab/ erry body saying dab."The Sound system continued to blast.

Rudy stepped out of the whip fresh as ever wearing a *Messian Margiela* shirt and pants with a pair of *Christian Louboutins* on his feet. At that point the energy changed.

"What's popping fellas?" *Rudy* said as he saluted the crowd.

"Us!" *Rico* said as he greeted *Rudy* with the infamous hood handshake.

"I know y'all heard about my party at *Club Mansion* tonight! Shit it's going to be some bad bitches floating around too, so who gone pull up?" Rudy said as he scanned the crowd.

"Me and Deon are definitely going to be there, especially since there's going to be some bad bitches there! Who's trying to miss that?" *Fernando* said as he grabbed the blunt back from *Meathead.*

The blunt was down to a roach size by that time, and as soon as *Fernando* grabbed the blunt gunshots rang out. "Pop, Pop, Pop, Tat, Tat, Tat!"

Everyone ran for cover as the semi-automatic weapon unloaded shots. *Fernando* held his Glock 40 in his hand as he crouched down beside *Meathead's* two door Audi coupe. He looked around searching for a shooter, but the crowd was scared and there was no way anyone could tell who the shooter was unless they were standing close by the shooter or the one being shot at. Car doors were rapidly closing as individuals scattered and tried to get the hell out of the way. Fernando looked over his shoulder at Dion and was signaling him to get up. He ran and crouched down back near his SUV. When the close was clear he and Deon eventually sped off.

"Bro you seen that shit?" Deon asked as he seemed to be out of breath.

"Hell naw I wasn't looking, I was running." Fernando shouted

"You must have seen who was spraying right?" Fernando yelled

"All I know is when I turned my head them niggas started airing out the crowd!" Deon replied as he lit up another blunt.

"I think they were Rudy's bloodhounds!" Fernando said

"Bro we on the same page."Deon said

Fernando nodded, hit the weed and said, "But yeah Deon, them fools ain't got no leash around their necks. Rudy got them niggas trained to go everyday all day!"

"I know right!" Deon says and closes his eyes trying to hold in the smoke.

Deon starts choking.

"Damn fool whoa! cough bro, cough."Fernando said while shaking his head.

"You good fam? Fernado said as he Patted Deon on the back.

"Bro you better drink some of that spring water before you choke to death." Fenando says.

"I'm good Nando! That shit blowing though."Deon said

"Tell me something I don't know!" Fernando added.

"But are we still fucking with the Mansion tonight?" Deon asked

"Come on bro are you for real? Cuz you know damn well I ain't trying to miss out on kicking it with some bad bitches!" Fernando said.

"Well you know where we need to be heading today." Deon implied

"I see you ain't been paying attention to the road." said Fernando pointing at the highway sign.

"Lennox mall!" Deon says slowly

"I'm glad we're on the same page cuz, because I done messed up my Tru's ducking them bullets."Deon continued

NORTH OF ATLANTA carries two of the most elegant shopping malls in the city. *Lenox Mall* and *Phipps Plaza* have a five-star rating when it comes to shopping for designer wear, and the chance to meet the who's who in the city. Fernando and Deon pulled up to the valet in front of Lenox They exited the vehicle and entered the spacious glass doors of the Lenox. The mall was laced with big spenders, sexy females and others who were waiting on their moment to catch both. While money was being spent and the females looked sexy and anticipated stumbling on a few blue hunduns. That delayed some of the goons that were lurking and laying on their next victim for a come up. Luckily Fernando and Deon were closely associated with the predators.

*John Legend* was a hustler who loved shopping at the mall. He worked the streets with the sole purpose of illuminating his surroundings. He checked character, and thought process and he was East side to death. He and Fernando bumped heads back in the sandbox while growing up. Because of the reputation that both of their father's held in the streets, John Legend and Fernando had no choice but to link up and work together, and fortunately there was no bad blood between the two of them.

"Hold on one second Deon." Fernando said as he crossed the walkway into the crowded section of people.

"Wazaam *Lil Rod*!"Fernando said

"Wazaam Nando!"*Lil Rod* responded.

After the greeting, they both dappped each other up.

"Whoa, Nando. Nigga your ass been MIA! You must don't fuck wit the MOB no more or something? And if you don't I don't give a fuck nigga, cuz you still my brother!" Legend said.

"Hey man! Don't do that fam! I'm the same nigga and ain't nothing change. We still family. Shiiiiiit I just be coolin bro."Fernando responded

Fernando continued, "I'm glad that you popped up cuz. I got some information that I know is going to tighten you up, and whatever you decide to do with it make sure that you fucks with ya boy. I ain't fucked up about no money, but when you get a wiff of this shit I know you gone cash out, and ain't no way in hell I'm going to let that cheddar go to somebody else."

Legend shakes his head up and down acknowledging what he heard and says. "Here's my number, hit me up sometime tomorrow."

He looked around from his left to his right and said. "This ain't the time, nor place for us to talk."

Fernando gave him a pound then walked off thinking anxiously about what was just told to him in bits and pieces. He canceled his thoughts, got his emotions in check and resumed his scheduled stroll through Lenox Mall.

He and Deon walked through the mall and headed towards Fernando's favorite store, *Louis Vuitton.* Regulars such as Fernando received presidential service upon entering a store like *Louis Vuitton.* A membership card was shown and customer service escorted him to a screen where he scanned it for the latest fashion and the service representatives complimented him with a fluke of *Louie XlII.*

"Hey Deon. Check out these scarfs and hats. I'm definitely feeling this black and yellow one."

"Nando, these boots will set your fit off bro."Deon exclaimed.

"Let me see, yeah I agree. Hit the buy button on those."Fernando said.

"I'm straight, have you grabbed everything you need it?"Deon continued.

"Yeah! I put a few items in the shopping cart.."Deon replied slowly.

"Okay hit the buy button, let's cash out and bounce. This Louie got me feeling good!"Fernando boasted.

Deon pressed complete on the screen and then gave the scanner to Fernando. He put his credit card information. The customer service rep came out with their bags within 5 minutes. Just below the cash register was a glass jewelry case, it had sport watches, bracelets, pendants and iced out dog chains in it. Fernando noticed a *Louis Vuitton* watch with a black band and canary yellow diamonds in the bezel. Deon looked at it and then gave Fernando the thumbs up.

Fernando thought about purchasing the watch but when he checked his G-Shock watch he said, "Bro time is flying. Are you good with everything you picked out?. Do you need anything else?"

"Naw I'm good fam. I appreciate the gear too."Deon said.

"Shiit ain't no pressure bro you good! Aight let's go!" Fernando responded.

"I need to get in touch with Nard before we get too late cuz you know how them old school niggas be acting when it get dark. Fernando continued.

"Shiit y'all was dead serious about snatching up some of that *Moon Rock* huh? Deon asked.

"Hell yeah Deon! Man ever since we smoked that first blunt, I've been higher than a mutherfucka!" Fernando said as they walked towards the valet parking.

NOT LONG AFTER leaving Edgewood, Fernando called Nard to let him know that he was on the way. Nard had been dealing with Fernando because of his father's connection and status. Fortunately for Deon he was blessed with the same treatment on the strength of Fernando.

As a business owner Nard stayed busy attending his affairs at the club in the West-End area of Atlanta. Whenever he was not pointing fingers, giving orders or directing the 50 lbs of work that came in once a month at the club, he would be rebuilding car motors and restoring the exterior of the vehicles for his collection in the backyard of his home.

Fernando pushed his ride with confidence and caution. He was ready to meet Nard and handle his business, he turned left off of Candler road into the *Tony Valley* community. He circled the block twice just to make sure that he wasn't being followed by any of the jack boys. Nard kept an old Chevrolet Blazer parked out on the front lawn with the 8-ft fence that squared the rear of his house.

Nard met him at the door, and led him to the rear of the house to a room that was insulated from the floor to the ceilings around the walls. There were piles of vacuum sealed bags stacked in the corner. Because of all of the work stacked to the ceiling Fernando knew that Nard had just reed-up on his inventory. Nard took out a pocket knife after grabbing one of the bags. He cut a hole wide enough to take out a few buds.

"Now this is the real deal here boy. I ain't never seen nothing like this and I'm talking about never!" Fernando said

"Yeah homie! This is what they call the top of the line shit.!" Nard said confidently

"I don't mean to cut you off, but why the price so high?" Fernando asked

"Believe me, I asked the same question at first. But once I seen this shit and what it do, oh man! The ticket wasn't even an issue no more!" Fernando exclaimed

Nard proceeded to cut a bigger hole in the bag, dumping the rest of the weed on the desk.

"So what are you trying to get?" Nard asked.

Fernando slowly shook his head and said, "Shiiiiit, if the price is right, I need like three bags. If not, just sell me a couple grams."

"Check this out. I normally charge eight g's for one, but since it's you, just give me six a piece."

"Say no more! Do you have your laptop close by?" Fernando asked quickly, not wanting to let the opportunity pass him by.

"Let me grab it from the bedroom. Give me one minute." Nard says.

Fernando linked his account, and then transferred $18,000 to Nard's business account. To make things look good at the end of the day, Nard prints out a receipt as if Fernando had purchased one of his hot old school hot rods.

The art of hustling was shown to Fernando at a young age,and to still have old heads like Nard lacing him with the sauce kept him on his a-game. Nard vacuum sealed each pound of weed together. Fernando took his package in his YSL bookbag and took off back to his side of town to separate the pack and roll up something to smoke and then get ready for a night on the town at *Club Mansion.*

# CHAPTER 2

## Club Mansion

FERNANDO AND DEON definitely made their presence known as they pulled up to the club. There were old school whips such as 1976 Cutlass 442's and 1967 Camaros that blended in the parking lot. There were also several foreign cars, such as California Ferraris, Rolls Royce Wraiths and a few Mercedes SL 550s.

The fashion that trended the VIP line had women in *Oscar Dela Renta* mini skirts, *Valentino* shoes and *Dolce and Gabbana Perfume* that scented their bodies. Inside the club, *Meathead*, *Rico*, and *Mexico Ran* was on stage performing the hit '*Dirty Sprite* ', and they had the crowd going crazy.

Meathead gestured with his hands for the crowd to be quiet. The crowd silenced and listened as Meathead said, "I just want to let y'all niggas know that we doing this shit for all my dawgs that's fucked up in the chaingang behind the wall. Shout out to my dawg Violatior, Man-Man, Woo, Jakari, and Dunnie- Man this shit crazy how they got my dawgs down bad. Free my niggas! DJ crank that shit back up!" Meathead screamed as he went back into beast mode performing Dirty Sprite.

The whole stage was filled with *Meatheads* entourage wearing fitted black T- shirts with *Lil Mexico's* logo printed on the front and a Mexican flag on the back.

The top section of the VIP area, housed some of the most exotic black, white and hispanic models that the club had to offer. Fernando and Deon weaved their way up to theVIP area that had a sign that read, "Reserved for Zone 6 only"

"Aye Nando!" Deon yelled over the music. "That boy *Rudy* wasn't bull shitin about the hoes. They everywhere!"

"Straight up! I got my eyes set on that caramel skin senorita over there. I wonder if Ma Mi tryin to take me to Mexico!" Fernando implied then gave_Dion a ziplock bag.

"What you waiting on my nigga! Roll up Shawty!" Fernado continued

"You better be glad I brought some more weed," said Deon.

Fernando looked at him with a blank expression.

"You must have forgotten about the THC Gel?" Nard said.

Fernando only shook his head in embarrassment.

"I can't even lie that shit slipped my mind bro. Now I have to go grab me a couple bags just to smoke."

"Shawty, you must have brought more than one?"

"Hell yeah, I brought three."

"Well roll up, and let's hit up this crowd and see what it do. Plus I'm trying to pull up on Rudy to let bro know that we showed up! Hold on real quick. there bro go over there by the bar!"Fernando said and grabbed some napkins and put about 7 grams on it.

Deon just stood there, checking out the honey's.

Fernando approached Rudy and said, "What it do my nigga! Shawty you got this spot on Fo Hunnid! There's bitches everywhere you turn!"

"Fam you know I wouldn't have no other way! I'm glad you showed up! Did Deon come wit you?" Rudy said with excitement.

"Yeah bro is up in the VIP area with the bitches. Aye *Rudy* here go you a little some that I want you to check out." Fernando said

"What the hell kind of weed is this? This shit looks like mothballs, but it smells good!" Rudy added, then placed the napkin in his pocket.

"If you like it, I got plenty more where that came from good buddy." Fernando said

"Bet that up fam! Hey, give him one of the bottles out of my case." Rudy said to the bartender.

"That's love. but I'll catch up with you later,"Fernando said.

ON THE WAY BACK across the dance floor Fernando ran into Nicole. She had already spotted him at the bar so she just sat back and waited on her moment.

"Oops I'm sorry for running into you." Nicole said as she looked up like it was a coincidence.

"Shawty, you must be following me?" Fernando said

She grabbed his hand and led him to the restroom section.

"Now that's more like it. I hate trying to yell over that loud ass music. But to answer your question, no I'm not following you, we just seem to always end up in the same spot."

"Are you here by yourself?" he asked.

"Yeah. You must be trying to do something later." Nicole asked

"I might. I just ain't got time for no problems that's all." Fernando explained

"Ain't gone be no problems because I'm as single as I can be as of tonight."

Nicole put her lips to his ear and continued, "Just so you know I'm wit whatever you wit."

"Aight you know where I'm kicking it at? Stop by before you leave and scream at me, so I can let my homie know what's up. "Fernando said, as he pointed upwards towards the VIP area.

"Okay. I wouldn't miss this for nothing."Nicole said as she walked off, giving Fernando a full view of what she had in store for him.

Deon was surrounded by three well stacked Hispanic girls when Fenando walked up. The women were all giggling while touching and grabbing his shirt. Deon motioned for Fernando to come and join him between the ladies.

"Papi, you bought a bottle for us?."Fernando grinned and then shook up the bottle and popped the cork.

The alcohol from the bottle soaked her face and breasts which only made the mamasita even more ready for what the night would bring.

"Papi, you know what we do to bad guys?"

Fernando shrugged his shoulders up and down. She leaned closer to his ear and whispered something then licked his earlobe.

"Word!"He turned his attention towards Deon and continued. "Bro, we need to wrap this shit up, cuz shawty talking about fucking the both of us!"

Deon laughed at Fernando's eagerness to leave.

Before Fernando had come back to the VIP area, Deon had blessed each of the females with a band of hundreds.

"You laughing my nigga, shit I'm trying to hit up the Doubletree,"Fernando exclaimed.

"My bad big homie! It's your call. I'm ready whenever you are ready."Deon responded.

Fernando stood up on the couch and locked eyes with Nicole. He played it off as if he was stretching and sat back down.

"Damn! I forgot all about Nicole" Fernando said

Deon gave him a puzzled look and said, "What the hell shawty got to do with these three beautiful Mamacita's right here?"

"Ole girl just pulled up on me out of the blue and said she trying to stroll wit me tonight,"said Fernando.

"Man! If that nigga *Rich Boy* finds out, he's going to kill the both of y'all. And on tha real fam, she ain't worth the time nor trouble that comes with fucking with her. Then you got…"Deon paused when Nicole became visible and waved at the ropes that lined the VIP area.

Fernando said, "I'll be right back as he walked towards Nicole thinking to himself, "Wazaam damn shawty fine!"

"I was just checking on you, and hoping that your company wasn't trying to spoil our night." Nicole said.

"Naw not really. But Deon just let me know that he and his homegirls were about to hit the doubletree. I was just about to pull up on you and see if you wanted to ride?"

"Naw, I'm straight on that, but I guess we'll see what tomorrow brings. See you later,"Nicole said and walked off.

Her last comment made Fernando wonder what Nicole was really all about. Fernando's thoughts were disrupted when his attention was suddenly drawn to Rudy and his dogs stomping some dude out in the corner. Fernando made his way back to the VIP, and told Deon and the females that it was time to go. So they exited the building and headed to their cars.

THE DOUBLETREE HOTEL had International flags attached to it that filled the skyline and blew with the wind. A bellman stood positioned on the red carpet at the Hotel's entry. Inside the hotel's foyer were gold railings on the spiral staircase and beautiful chandeliers in the high ceilings. The dining area also had an elegant touch and the menu consisted of the finest Mediterranean food. There was a Japanese portion of the menu for sushi lovers. You also had the option to have one of their top chefs personally come to your room and crank up a fiery flame on a grill that could bring your food to life right before your eyes.

Fernando chose to stay in the penthouse suite for the night. As soon as he and the females entered the spacious room, each one of them stripped down to their birthday suits. The room had a balcony that gave you a gorgeous view of some of Atlanta's nearby business districts. On the rooftop was a jacuzzi surrounded by a beautiful rosary garden with a spectacular 360 degree view of the College Park area.

The girls played in the water, smoked a blunt and drank *Patrone* out of wine glasses. One of the ladies had an ass like *Blac Chyna.* She stepped out of the jacuzzi and grabbed Fernando's arm gesturing for him to follow her back into the bedroom. She was ready for some action.

"Aye Papi. Can I ask you something?"

"I'm all ears, sexy mama. Fernando replied in a smoothed tone.

She pushed him back onto the bed, then straddled him on his lap.

"Mi love pain, I need you to make me scream. Can you make me happy Papi?"

"Yeah baby as long as you can handle this dick, because I'm ready to take you for a ride!"Fernando responded.

She reached in her bag and came out with a bottle of "*Kay Y*" jelly. Fernando had his mind made up, because if pain was what she wanted, then pain was what she was about to get. She took him deep into her mouth. Fenando grabbed her by her hair and deep throating her making her gag once.

"Awwh! Damn ma you doing that shit! Yeah, keep doing it just like that. Fuck yeah!"He moaned.

After slobbing on his manhood for a while covering it with her saliva, she was ready for some pounding. So she took a handful of Kay Y jelly and massaged it up and down the shaft of his dick. She stood up and squatted down on top of him but it caught Fernando by surprise when she inserted him into her back door.

"Do you like it, Papi? You like my Cula?" She said as her eyes rolled to the back of her head while taking every inch of him. She rocked back and forth giving him the opportunity to dig inside of her as deep as he could.

"Yes! Yes! More! More! I want more Papi! Aaaaahhhh oooooh!" she screamed.

Her rhythm and screams had Fernando about to explode, so he switched positions and put her on her hands and knees. Fernando used both of his hands and spread each of ass cheek. He inserted his manhood into her with a strong and wild thrust, and she started throwing it back and demanded for him to slap her on her ass.

And he did just that. Smack! Smack! Smack! was all you heard as he laid hands on her ass cheeks aggressively. Fernando tried playing with her pussy as he continued digging her back out, but she pushed his hand to the side, and replaced it with a vibrating bullet. The vibrator made her squirt every time he went harder and faster. The others couldn't help but to hear the screaming, so they came inside to be nosey. The other two women went and hopped in the bed. And for the rest of the night each of them let Deon and Fernando take turns drilling every hole that their bodies possessed.

ONCE DAYBREAK CAME, Fernando awoke to the smell of breakfast cooking. He looked over at Deon who was still knocked out cold from the extravaganza the night before. All three females were in the kitchen fully dressed.

"Wake up! Hey fool, wake up!" Fernando screamed while giving him a few nudges.

Deon jumped up looking around in shock. "What's wrong bro is everything straight!?"

"Yeah my nigga, but it's check out time!" Fernando screamed.

"Are y'all hungry?" One female said from the kitchen.

"I know damn well……Deon said in a confusing, and drowsy tone of voice.

Ferando noticed that he needed to calm him down so he said, "If you are looking for our sexy ladies from last night, well….

Fernando pointed towards the kitchen and continued, "I don't know about you, but I'm about to go eat."

Fernando proceeds to the kitchen following the aroma from the smell of the breakfast.

"Good morning Papi. I hope you slept okay? Si?"

Fernando nodded in agreement.

"Papi, I'm *Jennifer*, and that's *Carmine* and *Martina*."

Each female waved and smiled at Fernando.

"Just thought we should introduce ourselves, since you strong men worked so hard last night."

"Well I'm Fernando, and that's my boy Deon."

Deon stood at the kitchen door, and saluted.

“Fernando! Are you mixed? Half and half? No Poppi?”Carmine questioned.

“Naw baby. I ain’t mixed, if that’s what you mean that’s just my street name.” Fernando responded.

“Okay, Papi since we all know each other now, are me and my friends going to see y’all again?” Jennifer asked.

“Mamicita, we are definitely going to keep in touch,” Fernando spoke with excitement as he finished his breakfast.

They all exited the hotel and headed to the valet. Fernando gave his ticket to the attendant. After a few minutes of waiting, the valet walked up to him with an uneasy look on his face.

Fernando became concerned.

“What’s going on? Bra,where my shit at?”Fernando asked forcefully.

“Sir, I’m terribly sorry but all of your tires have been cut. Give me one second, and let me get the manager for you.”

The kid ran off.

“I know that’s right! Somebody better come tell me some like asap!”Fernando shouted.

“You believe this? What kind of funny shit going on around here?”Fernando continued.

“I don’t know Nando, but this shit crazy!”Deon said.

“Excuse me sir.”The manager said as he checked the ticket. “Mr. White, we’re really sorry for the inconvenience. We’ve already notified the police and our insurance will cover all of your damages,”the manager continued.

“So how in the hell am I supposed to get home then?”

“Like I, we are here to assist you on whatever you need.”The manager said. “There’s a tow truck on the way for your vehicle, and we have a rental car service on the way for you as well. You will be all squared away shortly sir.”He continued assuring Fernando.

The rental service arrived a few minutes after the tow truck pulled off. Deon knew Fernando was blowed, so he suggested that if Fernando wanted to just go straight home then he would just kick it at his spot.

As soon as Fernando got into the house he went straight to the shower. Deon on the other hand was busy hooking up the movie projector. Deon heard Fernando's phone ringing and he glanced over at the front screen. Nicole's name appeared next to five missed calls along with one from Don Legend.

Several text messages also scrolled across the screen of his phone. Deon read a few of them, but when he heard the shower cut off, he placed the phone back on the table. He thought his eyes were tripping at what Nicole was saying in her text messages. From the looks of the text messages, she seemed to be an unidentified stalker.

"Nando bro your phone has been blowing up!"

"I hope it's them folks saying they got my shit right."Fernando said as he looked at his phone screen.

"What the hell! Shawty straight up tripping for real!" He screamed.

"What's going on fam?" Deon asked

"This bitch Nicole, she sent all kinds of stupid ass text messages." Fernando said and then tossed his phone to Deon so that he could see.

"Yeah bro. I see. She on some other shit!"

"You think she's the one that cut your shit up?" Deon asked.

"Ain't no telling. But I'm going to find out though!" Fernando said.

"All I'm going to tell you is to be careful bro, because messin wit old girl, you ain't gone do nothing but bring some extra heat on yourself trust me." Deon said with a serious look on his face.

"True. Well, I'll handle it later. What the hell you got playing on the big screen?" Fernando asked.

"This is a classic called *Blue Hill Avenue.* Ain't nothing but some gangster shit going on on this show. But shiiiit we might as well chill and smoke up the rest of this *Moon Rock* until dem folks call about your ride." Deon said with a grin on his face.

"Ain't no pressure bro, but we are going to smoke like grown folks today."

Deon gave Fernando a puzzled look.

"Yeah buddy. We bout to get high today." Fernando says and started stuffing weed in his personal bong pipe.

"It's Friday. We ain't got no job and we ain't got shit to do!"he said trying to give his best Chris Tucker impression.

Deon clutched his stomach laughing as hard as he could.

"Finish that off, while I make this call bra,"Fernando said as he hit redial on his phone, and headed up to his bedroom.

The phone rang three times and then Don Legend answered saying, "Whoa what's up?"

"What the hell you got going on bro? Fernando said

"Waiting on you. Is you somewhere by yourself so that we can talk?"Don Legend asked.

"Hell yeah. And you need to spill them beans, cuz this shit been riding my mind like a mother fucker."Fernando said anxiously.

He was paying full attention to what was about to be said.

"You remember *Ricardo* that used to run with your pops back in the day?"

"Yeah. *Ricardo* from *East Lake Meadows*. What about him?"Fernando said as his curiosity was killing him.

Don Legend continued, "Last week, me and some of my people did a kick door. Just so happened the spot was Ricardo's son, *Lil Nick*. But to make a long story short, after we tortured shawty for about 30 minutes straight asking for the safe, this lil hoe finally told us that *Ricardo* keeps all the cash at his spot. This nigga so flaky, that he put it on his life that there wasn't no cash there, and then he gave us the address to his pops spot. He was so scared he started rambling on about his dad and how much money he had over at his spot. And then he came out his mouth sideways. This nigga said that his dad was paid a hundred racks to knock off your pops."

Fernando stood holding the phone and felt rage building on the inside. He was lost for words after what he had just heard.

He had no feelings at that moment, no expression, and everything was blank. He blacked out for a moment.

"Snap out of a J.R.,"Don Legend said.

Fernando snapped out of it and returned back to the real world.

"So what y'all did with Lil Nick?"

"Not over the phone bro. But wazaam Nando? Is everything a green light?" Don Legend asked.

"0-4."Fernando said and hung up.

Now he was faced with a new dilemma. But this burden wasn't one that would hang around for long. Fernando knew how his people rolled. When Don Legend did his thing, shit got done asap, and without giving the situation another thought, he remembered who he was dealing with. Once the call finally came in, he knew that he would be at peace.

Fernando looked up towards the sky and said to himself. "I got you pops. On God I got you Pops."

# CHAPTER 3

## In the Heart of Moment

C*layton County*, better known as *Clayco.* To the average eye, there is not a whole lot going on in that part of the city. Ricardo worked *The Underground Railroad* in the streets. That was the name it was given. That was because there was a lot of unseen trapping, trafficking, and money laundering that went on in *The Underground Railroad.* Ricardo crept through the streets of *Atlanta*, and played by the old school rules. When the street lights came on, the traps were sealed up, and if you wasn't a regular customer, ain't no way you was about to get served.

Ricardo checked each camera and then grabbed a strap before heading to his garage. As soon as he opened the side door, there was an unusual smell.

"I must be out of gas?"He questioned himself, looking around before entering his SL550 Mercedes Benz. Once he turned the ignition on, the person who was lurking in the back seat of the vehicle appeared from the shadows.

"We are going to take everything slow from here on out. Turn this bitch off and keep them hands where I can see em mutherfucker!"

Ricardo's hands shook nervously. He thought about going out like a *G,* but he second guessed his decision once he caught a glimpse of the masked gunman in his rearview mirror . There is a theory that some people think that if the robber doesn't show their face, then that means they're most likely going to live. However that theory has not always reigned true.

"Youngin, just tell me what you want and it's yours!"Ricardo pleaded.

"Whenever you meet up with that rat ass son of yours tell him thank you!"

"Pop! Pop!"

Don legend wiped down everything, He emptied Ricardo's pockets and secured his mask. He dumped the rest of the gas out of the container on the inside of the Mercedes before running through the house and looking for anything else of value.

TWO HOURS LATER..,....

"Where the fuck is my phone? Fernando patted his bed. Bingo."He saw the back pocket of his pants light up as they laid on the chair.

"Hello," he answered.

"Shit good around my way. Pull up on me later."John legend ended the call.

He knew that his homeboy was about to ask a million questions. He made away with 10 lb of gas and a brick of heroin. He knew it was more where that came from, however he just didn't have time to get it.

MONIQUE HAD BEEN spending more nights away from home with her boyfriend. Her mother, Tina went out and found herself a driver to run her around the city to go shopping, eat dinner, and sometimes go to a movie. That had become her normal routine. Once Reggie came into the picture, the times Monique and Tina used to sit at home and have girls talk or have the driver take them shopping came to an end. Reggie was a graduate of Emory University, and the lead brain surgeon at Grady Memorial Hospital. His salary is upwards of $250,000 a year, and that number was right up Monique's alley.

Alex the driver eventually became Tina's substitute for companionship. There would be times when they would drive around the city until nightfall just to keep Tina company. Other than going their separate ways, work went from 6:00 o'clock in the evening until whenever.

Alex is a convicted felon who's been home for 3 years after serving a 17 year bid. He's 45 with a prison yard body. Alex and Tina discussed each other's past during their first conversation. The news left Tina in shock. She couldn't believe that he had been to prison. As they continued to talk, Tina noticed how his life was similar to her late husband the infamous *Frank White*, the only difference was he was not as wealthy. Tina respected a man who lived for his family. As they listened to Teddy Pendergrass songs it had Tina and Alex in a daze reminiscing down memory lane.

Alex remembered the time when he was brought back to his cell from Court after being sentenced. He called home to find out that his wife was gone. It took her less than 2 weeks, and she was renting a house on the other side of town. When she moved, she only took what she and her boys needed. Within a month's time, he received a letter in the mail informing him that their marriage was over. Decisive, pragmatic, and cold was her way of handling things.

Alex went from a well known hustler to a nobody…a has been, in no time. Prison had become his future home and he didn't have a dime to his name. He asked himself, "Was that the life that he wanted?"

Alex was broken from his stupor and unhappiness once he looked up at Tina's face. He smiled at the site of her. After he continued to explain how his wife ran off with the kids and his money, that opened the door for Tina to lend an ear for his pain. And he was definitely in pain from the tramas that he had faced. However, today Tina wanted to do more than just sit around and share stories.

"Are you okay Alex?"Tina asked, sensing that his mind was elsewhere.

"Yeah I'm good, boss lady,"Alex responded.

"What did I tell you about that boss lady mess, that makes me feel old," Tina said.

"Excuse me then Ms. Tina!"Alex responded.

"Now that's more like it," she said and checked her watch.

"Are you hungry?" Tina asked.

"You know I'm a country boy, we never get full,"Alex said.

"Well, put Houston's restaurant into your GPS system and let's get going, because I'm starving," Tina added.

On the way to the restaurant, Alex and Tina had their regular debate about the NBA. She's a *Kobe* fan and he's a ride or die *LeBron* fan, they stayed going at it. Alex turned off of Peachtree Street into the restaurant. He stopped at the front entrance and let the valet handle the rest. They entered the restaurant and the host seated them and took their orders. The gorgeous scenery and extreme beauty that Tina displayed under the burning candle on the table had Alex mesmerized.

"This is a really nice place. I could definitely get used to this kind of dining."Alex said.

"You mean to tell me that you have never been to Houstons before?" Tina asked Alex as she waved for the waiter to come.

Alex held an embarrassing look on his face. He shook his head from left to right.

"Tina, back when I was doing my thing most of the money that I made went into the family savings, and like I told you before, I mainly hustled for them."Alex said as he stared into space. His mind started remembering the past.

"I'm sorry if I offended you,"Tina said as she reached for his hand.

"I told you I'm trying to work on that. There's nothing to be sorry about. Tina I'm fine, that's what we're here for right?"

"I guess so."

2 hours later, they finished up the night with two shots of Patrone and one Margarita. It was Tina's choice. The alcohol started to take an effect on her. Tina grabbed his hand and placed her head on his shoulder.

"It's getting late. I think we need to be getting you home young lady,"Alex said.

"Alex, you sound like my father."Tina said.

"God bless the dead, and don't let me sound like a party pooper. Okay then so where to next?"Alex asked.

"I figured since Monique was gone for the weekend, that we could go back to the house, relax, and probably have a few more drinks. What do you think?"Tina suggested.

"Boss lady, I'm all for it! Oops my bad Tina!"Alex jokingly said.

Alex began driving towards Tina's house. He could tell that Tina was feeling herself, because during the entire drive home she couldn't keep her hands off of him. When they arrived, Tina walked into the house, and headed straight to the bar and opened a bottle of white Remy. Alex had never taken her for much of a drinker. However, once he saw Tina began to drink directly from the bottle and approaching him in a sexually aggressive manner, Alex knew it was on and that the liquor was getting the best of her.

"Let's go out by the pool. It's too hot in here, and I need some fresh air,"She said.

Alex followed her lead. The Remy made Alex see Tina in a different light. It gave him a special feeling for her and had Alex looking at Tina not as his boss, but more of a sexy, lovely woman in his eyes. Alex had always seen her as an attractive older woman, but flirting with the boss was something that he could never afford to do because he was now steadily employed with her and he didn't want to jeopardize that.

Tonight was different. Alex and Tina had connected in a way as if him being labeled as her personal driver never existed.

"Tina, you have a beautiful home. Everything is set up perfect for the queen that you are. And not to forget a sexy Queen,"Alex stated.

Tina rose from her seat, and went and sat on Alex's lap. She took his wine glass from his hand and finished it off herself then threw the flute on the grass. She kissed him. Alex became aroused. He lifted her up and positioned her so that she was facing him. His hands traveled her body from her breast to the bottom of her ass cheeks. Tina was in pure ecstasy as she began to grind on his lap.

"Let's take this upstairs. My pussy can't take this no more!"she aggressively implied.

"Ladies first."Alex gestured with his hand.

Tina grabbed a hold of his hand and up the stairs they went. She led him to the guest room on the second floor. The master bedroom was off limits. It was too early in their encounters for Alex to have the privilege to invade her living quarters because this was their first time.

Alex took charge and laid Tina on the bed and began slowly undressing her. Tina moaned. Alex teased her pussy with his thumb by rubbing it against her clit. He was blowing and fingering her pussy at the same time. Alex had a few skills in the bedroom and he knew that he had to use all he had to please this more experienced woman.

Tina took short intense breaths, and cried out . "Please! I need you inside of me."

Alex strapped on a condom. He was about to enter her walls but she stopped him and slid the condom back off.

"My tubes are tied, so you ain't gotta worry about that."she said with a smile.

Tina spread her legs as wide as she could, and Alex slid his manhood all the way into her wetness.

"Ooooh yes! Right there Alex! Right there!"she screamed.

Her pussy creamed all over his dick while he grinded from side to side trying to explore every inch of her insides. Alex felt his dick head swell up so he pulled back. In order to not cum quick, Alex switched positions and flipped Tina on her stomach.

Tina reached back, slapping her big ass and anxious for him to enter her. He entered her wetness and began digging deep inside of her walls. The faster he went the more nut came from Tina's pussy. She arched her back, allowing him the access to travel further inside of her. They switch positions a few more times during their rendezvous. Alex couldn't take it any more.

He released his fluids inside of her. They laid still until both of them fell asleep.

MEET ME IN THE parking lot at South DeKalb Mall in 10 minutes. Fernando hit the end button on his car's touch screen. He prayed that this was it. Finally he felt closer to achieving his goal. All he kept saying to himself was, "Please let this be it, please let this be it!"

He drove in silence, there was no music or anyone else with him. It was just him and Fifteen Thousand in cash.

The mall was not crowded like it normally was. Fernando parked beside Don Legend's tinted out Chevrolet Malibu. There were no words uttered, it was just an even exchange of Nike duffle bags. They parted ways, not even looking back until they met up again.

# CHAPTER 4

## Family Over Everything

REGGIE LIVES ON Northside Drive, behind a fifteen foot black gate with a courtyard that circled around a cupid fountain statue that stood just a few feet away from the front door. The European style home had a floral garden and ivory vines for siding on the house.

Around 1 a.m. that morning, Reggie was called to the emergency room. Monique had been up all night waiting on his return. For the past few weeks, he had been disappearing on the regular, mainly at night.

Her mind was made up, "Tonight, I need more verification than just a work number in his pager."

He turned the car lights off just as he pulled into his driveway. He cruised up to the front door. He noticed that the light in the family room was still on.

"It's 4:30 in the morning," he said to himself.

He grabbed his suitcase and prepared himself for the worst between him and Monique. He entered his dark estate and approached the family room where Monique sat with her arms folded staring at a blank TV.

"Baby are you okay?" Reggie asked

"Hell no, I'm not okay!" Monique shouted.

"Reggie I'm so sick and tired of this shit! Laying around here alone while you're out roaming the streets doing God knows what, and with who! I'm tired!" Monique continued.

What do you mean, roaming the streets? I've been at work all night Monique!"

"Oh yeah, well why when I called you around three this morning you were nowhere to be found, huh? Answer that!"Monique yelled.

Baby I was probably on break!

Monique shushed him with her hand.

"I tell you what, how about I take a break then!"Monique said as she brushed past Reggie moving fast towards the front door.

She stopped and lowered her head releasing a few tears as she snatched her keys from the key holder on the wall. Monique hit the road mad at Reggie and hurt as ever by his behavior towards her.

The sun crept over the clouds of the early morning skies, as Monique circled interstate 285. Once Monique finally arrived at her mother's house she wondered why her mother Tina didn't have the driver park inside of the garage. When Monique entered her mom's home she noticed that things were all out of place. The liquor and wine cabinet was left wide open, two wine glasses sat on the kitchen counter.

"Why is the back door open?" She said to herself.

Monique stormed upstairs to Tina's bedroom. It was empty. She called her name several times. There was no answer. Monique became suspicious and she almost panicked. She began checking every room in the house, and when she reached the fifth guest room, the door swung open and Monique was lost for words.

"Ma!" Monique screamed.

Tina rolled over staring at her daughter. She shook her head before sinking into the covers. Alex didn't know what to do. The situation was more of an embarrassment to him than anything.

"Ma. Can you please tell me why Alex is here and in your bed?" Monique said.

There was an oppressive silence that filled the room.

"He needs to go Ma! Like now!"Monique screamed.

"Monique you need to lower your tone, and while you're at it get out so we can put some clothes on!" Tina snapped.

Monique ran out, and slammed the door behind her. Moments later, Tina came down the steps in her robe. She found Monique in the kitchen sitting at the bar with a disappointed look on her face.

"Sorry for yelling at you. And as for Alex…Everything just happened so fast last night and one thing led to another. It really wasn't supposed to happen. But Monique, ever since you have been gone, I have just been…" Tina said.

She tried to touch her daughter's hand only to be rejected. This was something that Monique wasn't used to. Tina was about to continue explaining herself but then she figured that she needed some time to herself. Alex was able to sneak past the kitchen where only Tina could see him. Tina gave Alex a nod, signaling for him to keep going so that Monique couldn't see him. Alex left the house and fled the scene heading towards South Atlanta.

ALEX STEPPED INTO the front door of his place. There were piles of mail scattered on the carpet. Alex sat down and got comfortable and glanced through each envelope.

"Damn, Parole office!"He said to himself.

He knew that whenever they sent something by Express Mail, nine times out of ten it was about paying them some money. He couldn't really focus based on the situation that his boss lady just had him in. When he heard his phone ring he began patting his pockets to make sure that his phone was still in his pocket. By the time he realized where the phone was, it stopped ringing. He looked at his phone and noticed that there was a missed call from Tina with a text message coming through. It read:

"Alex, my daughter is very upset. SMH. I think it would be best if we gave her some time. You were my first since my husband's been gone, so I know that my kids may have a hard time with me seeing someone else right now. Things may be moving a little too fast for you also, so I understand why you may not want to talk. I'll send you a check for all your troubles and I'll enclose some extra for your time off. Bye.... Tina"

Alex lowered his head. Ever since he had been released from prison, he vowed to leave hustling behind him. He wanted to bury that habit with the system that tried its best to keep him locked behind the walls. And now that his gig with Tina was ending, he wasn't sure what he was going to do. Between having to pay parole fees and living, he knew that there was something different that had to be done.

A FEW DAYS later, Tina received a call from Alex asking her if he could come and pick up his final check. Tina agreed that he could stop by. However, Tina gave him instructions to wait outside. Monique was home at the time, and Tina didn't want to upset her again. Once Alex pulled up to Tina's house, she came out and gave Alex a look, showing him that his presence was missed.

"Are you mad at me?" Tina asked him with an uneasy tone.

"No, I am just more disappointed in myself to think that we could have actually gone somewhere with this." Alex responded.

Tina tried grabbing his hand to comfort him. Alex had a blank expression on his face, and he was so tense that he never loosened his tight grip of the steering wheel.

"Please don't be like that, I feel bad!"Tina whined like a little girl.

Alex silenced her by holding up one finger.

He closed his eyes, took a deep breath and said, "I think it's best for the both of us that we let things just be what they are, and if it's meant to be then we'll cross paths again."

Tina put her head down and turned to walk away. She took one last glance over her shoulder at Alex before he pulled off. Alex burned rubber out of the driveway leaving Tina very emotional. Monique had been looking out of the bedroom window the entire time and knew that Alex didn't take the encounter too well.

MONIQUE FLOPPED DOWN on her bed. She began thinking about Reggie and all of the wrong things she thought he had been doing, and because she didn't have full knowledge of everything it was eating alive, and she couldn't take it. She sat there thinking about how she couldn't ever imagine her father stepping outside of his relationship with her mother. That last thought pushed her mind into the direction of getting herself a new companion. Her train of thought was interrupted by her mom calling her. Monique ignored the call and acted as if she was asleep. There was too much going on, and she was dying to vent to someone.

THE SKIES SEEMED brighter, and the world was spinning at his fingertips.

"Blessings were coming in all shapes and forms," Fernando smiled and said to himself.

Fernando felt that today would be perfect for getting answers on how to deal with Nicole.

He drove on the interstate towards the westside of Atlanta to visit Amber. She worked with Nicole at the strip club and also did a little side work for Fernando. He got off Interstate 20 on exit 53 westbound and stopped at the red light on MLK.

Monique's name appeared on his touch screen dash.

"Hold on for a second sis. Let me pull over to the side of the road. I'm back. I pulled over into *Moseley Park*. So what's going on stranger?" Fernando said to his sister.

"J.R. Have you heard about your mother?" Monique said eagerly.

"Hold on sis. Slow down. Now what's going on with Ma? Ain't nobody told me shit!" He said in a confused tone of voice.

"Physically, she's fine bra, but Ma done lost her last damn mind messing around with Alex." Monique said.

"Oh yeah! What's wrong with Alex?" He asked, feeling a bit at ease.

"Come on J. R. I know damn well you don't approve of that?"

"Now I see what's going on. Is it because he don't make a quarter mill a year like you know who? Does that not mean he ain't good enough for Ma…huh? Sis let me tell you this! Money don't make a relationship." Fernando said.

"But J.R." Monique whined.

"Look sis, I'm good on this conversation. While you're so focused on that. Your brother got a real thin line between love and hate bitch chasing him around the city. And shawty done slashed all of my tires! So I ain't got time for that nonsense," Fernando told Monique.

"Whaaat! When did this happen?" She questioned.

He paused for a few seconds and Monique anxiously tapped her foot as she waited on a response.

"My people's calling in on the other line. Imma stop by and check on y'all later. And don't be over there stressing Ma out either!" Fernando said and quickly hung up the phone so that Monique couldn't distract him from his mission.

# CHAPTER 5

## West Side Chick

BY DAY SHE went by *Amber*, and when the night falls she's *Lady Ice.* At the age of thirty -four which is slightly over the age for a stripper, however, she carried a fabulous shape along with her gorgeous ebony skin. *Lady Ice* was also known for her expensive taste.

The relationship that she and Fernando had was mainly based strictly on business with the exception of their late night encounters, every now and then.

Fernando's first love was taking pictures and playing with cameras. Growing up, he took pictures of everything moving. Fernando's father *White* always told people that their last name would one day become a household name., thanks to his son. Fernando believed every word that his father spoke. Nowadays, Fernando used his camera to capture photos of the sexiest females in most of Atlanta's hottest strip clubs and then sell them to Urban magazines.

He eased past the *Washington High* night school's traffic and turned on the dead end street where *Amber* stood with her arms folded and a disappointed look on her face. She hopped in the front seat, with her eyes forward and arms still folded. He playfully pulled her arms loose.

She smirked and said. "I know next time right?"

"What?" Fernando responded.

"Nigga you said 30 minutes! It's been an hour and some! I bet next time I'll be getting ready in 30 minutes." She complained.

Fernando gave her the silent treatment.

"Why don't you put some rims on this porsche? It's already cute but some rims will make it sexy." *Lady Ice* asked.

"Why didn't you become a designer instead of a stripper?" He asked sarcastically.

"Sorry she replied. So what's good? What we got going today?" *Lady Ice* asked.

She hit the auto button to adjust the seat.

"Ain't no picture taking today girl. We got to sit down and have a talk about one of your co-workers. Her name is *Nicole*. Does that name sound familiar to you?"Fernando asked.

"*Nicole*?"Amber thought for a minute to herself.

"Yeah! *Nicole Parker*. She goes by, *Black Angel*."Lady Ice remembered.

Fernando shook his head and said, "Black Angel my ass. I believe shawty slashed my tires the other day. I know it had to her because I don't fuck with too many of them hoes like that. Now I remember old girl,"Amber said. Last week she was in front of the club arguing with some dread head nigga. That must have been her dude because after he got through chomping her ass off, she ended up in the front seat of his Lexus."

Amber locked her sights in on a blunt that was in the ashtray of Fernando's car and without asking, she grabbed it and fired it up.

"That can't be nobody but Rich boy."Fernando said as he pulled up at home.

"Grab my food off the back seat while I park,"he said as he hit the locks.

Lady Ice got out of the car at the entrance. She was still smoking. Fernando parked in his normal spot. For the remainder of the night, Amber filled him in on all of the information that she knew about Nicole and what the hood grapevine had been saying about the late Ricardo and his son, Lil Nick.

The sky had darkened by the time they finished eating. Fernando pondered on what the streets were saying. *Ricardo* killed *White* because he was a snitch. That had him fucked up, because never in a million years would anybody who knew *White*, think that he was a snitch.

Fernando needed answers and he figured that the only person he knew would keep it all the way real and uncut with him was Nard. He made a mental note that he was going to go and see him first thing tomorrow. Fernando kept all the pieces to the puzzle to himself about White.

He went back into the dining room and resumed his time with Amber. He finished clearing the dining room table off, while Amber sat on the Designer living room couch that he purchased from *Huff Furniture.* Amber somehow found Fernando's weed stash and began rolling up. Fernando looked at Amber and shook his head at *Miss Bloodhound.*

"Your phone vibrating!"She said.

"Toss it to me."Fernando responded.

Amber threw his phone to him and Fernando caught it. Nicole's phone number lit up on the screen. He started to put her to the test by letting Amber answer, but he thought against it, not wanting to detour his plan.

"You could have answered your phone. I hope you ain't worried about me?"Amber said.

"No it ain't that. That was your co- worker/psychopath calling."Fernando retorted.

"Nando, why don't you just give me the green light, and let this hoe know how a TTG bitch rocks. These shits ain't soft. This a hard body."Amber said, leaning back, giving Fernando a high five.

He shook his head and said. "You know that you're dead on going back to the west side tonight right?"

"So what are you trying to say, I got to sleep on the couch?" she asked.

"Yep!" he responded.

Amber threw a pillow at him.

Fernando dodged the pillow and said, "You good. You can get my room. I'm going to stay up a while to check on a few things online."

"Are you sure? I ain't gone front like this a bitch first time sleeping on the couch,"Amber asked.

"Shawty, you better take your butt on up dem steps before I get mad."He told her.

Lady Ice gave Fernando her middle finger and walked off.

Fernando went to his office, turned on the lights and sat down in front of his laptop. He began contemplating his approach about what he was going to say.

He thought hard about his upcoming discussion. He wanted to know when and how? Snitched on who? Those would be the main topics when he talked to Nard.

Fernando started responding to his site.There was one message that caught his attention. He knew that females would go to the extreme just to get the right amount of recognition and attention. Just like the particular site that read: "*Looking for models and dancers only.*"

The female responding to the site must have had the impression from seeing the homepage with a dude and his girlfriend surrounded by lights and cameras, that this was a dating site. Fernando had a bright idea. He decided to create a feint. He put "*Coming Soon.*" on the website and then set up a temporary template to let people know that dates were now available. He put his name at the top of the list of dates available.

His whole purpose for a dating site was to see how far Nicole would go to get with him, and Amber was his bait. His curiosity was killing him. After Fernando published the site, he shut everything down and headed for the shower. Before getting in the shower he peeked inside the bedroom at Amber, and she was out cold.

"That Moon Rock don't play!" He said to himself before he turned the lights off.

Fernando took a shower and smoked a blunt before laying down. He told Alexa to play the soothing sounds of Maxwell.

# CHAPTER 6

## Family Problems

WAKING UP TO 10 missed calls with a few unwelcoming text messages led Fernando to know that there were consequences at hand by not showing up the day before.

Monique was upset. He woke Amber up, got dressed, and left to get the day started. After dropping Amber off, he swung by the downtown Farmers Market on Auburn Avenue. He wanted to grab a few items for his mom. Afterwards, he went to the bakery to get her some donuts, which was Monique's favorite. He didn't want to know how his two favorite women would act if he showed up empty-handed, that answer was better untold and unseen.

While driving to his moms house, Fernando got an incoming call from *Mr Quick*. *Mr. Quick* was the man when it came to refurbishing old school cars. If you wanted a hot rod that was made to race and make you some money on the racetrack, then you took your car to *Mr. Quick*.

"Hey! What's going on, Old Man?"Fernando said when he answered the phone.

"Nothing much son, but the heat. It's hot as hell out here,"Mr Quick responded.

"I was just calling to let you know that I got you all wrapped up and ready to go."Mr. Quick continued.

"Aight bet! As soon as I leave my Mom Dukes house, I'm going to pull up!"Fernando said excitedly.

"Tell Mrs White I said hello, and I'll talk to you when you get here,"Mr Quick said and ended the call.

His next agenda didn't look too promising. There was a stretch of uncertainty that he felt in his body, as he stared at Nard's phone number. First and foremost, the truth was long overdue. And he did not want to waste another moment. Fernando dialed the number and the phone rang twice.

"Hello,"Nard answered.

"What's up old man? I was wondering if you weren't too busy. I need to scream at you face to face for a minute on a serious tip."Fernando said.

"I'm here,"said Nard." And watch your mouth with that old man shit, young nigga!"

Fernando was just turning on Candler Road, when he hung up the phone with Nard. This was worse than a cold case file. But one thing was for sure, the answer to the equation was about to be solved. *Knock, Knock, Knock.* The door swung open. Nard had a long blunt hanging from his lips with a shirt that read "*Rest In Peace Ricardo*"across the front of it. Seeing him wearing that shirt seemed strange to Fernando.

"Come on in Nando. You letting out all of my AC,"Nard said.

The living room was laced with plastic covered furniture like in the '70s. The light was dimmed with only a glare from the 72 inch smart TV. Nard tried passing Nando a blunt, but Fernando declined.

"What's on your mind?" Nard asked.

"A lot," said Fernando. And I really need you to give it to me raw and uncut bro. Because you're the only one who knows the truth. But before we start, I need to know everything.

"Hold on Nando! You got to tell me everything that's going on before you keep making all these demands,"Nard said hastily.

Fernando exhaled heavily and said, "What really happened with my father before he was murdered? Because I know Ricardo was paid to kill him."

Nard's expression said that he had some knowledge of what was just said.

"You might want to hit this blunt for this one Fernando,"Nard said.

"The year was 2012 and cocaine prices were at an all-time high. The plugs were either getting knocked off or moving away from Georgia. *El Helza*, who went by *Hell, was George's* main supplier. *Frank White* was copping 10 bricks and 10 bails of weed every week and so was *Nasty Red.* While everyone else stacked their paper and ducked off, *White* was said to be doing the most. His actions were being reported and that was the first mistake. After *Hell* received his last payment from *White,* he put him to the test. That was another move against *White.* Fulton Industrial Boulevard was well known for prostitution and drugs. *Babe's Strip Club* sat on the corner and also a meeting spot. *El Helza* was part owner of the club and he kept his product there inside a storage room. The normal procedure to get your drop was to catch a cab to the club, sit for 30 minutes at the bar, and then a minivan would be loaded up with the keys in the ignition waiting on you outside.

On this particular day, things were different and there had been a change of plans. White had always made his runs by himself however that day he had a feeling in his gut like he had never felt before. He sensed that something wasn't right as he drove. White noticed that all of the exit ramps that he passed had an officer blocking the entrance. His horrible gut feeling instantly became a reality when the officers had him cornered with nowhere to run.

The officers screamed, "Driver! Show me your hands! Now!"

While the officers screamed, yelled, searched the vehicle and then arrested White, all he could think about was losing everything including his family. The thought of that just kept replaying his mind. He tried to figure out who, how, and what led to this? Based on the way the meeting was set up, there was no way this could be happening. However, it was and he was being escorted to the crime unit in downtown Atlanta.

He was too embarrassed to say the least, and he couldn't let his wife know. There was too much at stake. He really was self-conscious about how Tina would take it. Once a person is placed in situations like this, it takes a strong mind, heart, and it requires the will to fight and overcome what seemed to be the end of the world, and trust me a lot of people aren't born with that type of heart, mindset or will power.

*White* eventually gave up the plug. Most people call it the game. One thing for sure is that the game can be played in a lot of ways, you can play sports, videogame or even the real world games. The game was being played on *White*. What was happening to him was all a charade at the hands of *El Helza* just to see if *White* was worth putting on the chopping block. This game that *El Helza* was playing had never failed him. He had others in the organization like *Ricardo*. He was getting money, just not on the same level as *White*. There was also *Nasty Red*, and *Nard*. But *Ricardo* was next in line and waiting for his moment to take *White's* place. When the call finally came in from the boss man after *White* snitched, *Ricardo* was ready to terminate White's call for duty. And he did just as he was ordered to do.

The passenger who was with White his last day on Earth, Nard, was left with a permanent scar, but was inducted into the Hall of Fame in El Helza's book for his role in the movie.

Right after the job was done, *Hell* moved back home to California. For their role in knocking *White* off, *Nasty Red*, *Ricardo,* and *Nard* didn't want for anything in the drug game.

Once Fernando heard Nard's name mentioned in the same sentence as White, it immediately put him on the defense, and before *Nard* knew it there were two punches coming his way.

"Pussy Nigga! Imma kill you!"Fenando yelled as he swung on Nard.

"Awwwwhhh!" Nard cried out after the two punches connected with his face.

"Listen man! Just listen to me!" Nard pleaded.

"Listen to what nigga! You helped them kill my father!" Fernando screamed. "And ain't nothing you can say to me man, and what the fuck was you thinking anyway?"Fernando continued and stepped forward towards Nard and then stopped.

NARD TRIED TO continue explaining. "You don't understand how dealing with the cartel is Nando, and if the shoe was on the other foot, trust me White would have done it to us. Then it would have been him doing it to us and then we would be dead. Listen Nando this game ain't made for the weak hearted. And did you hear what I said? Yo daddy gave up the plug! Y'all was lucky *Hell* didn't come at you, your sister, and mom. I know it might sound heartless but when dealing with somebody like El Helza, you have to stay on point, because that guy is connected with people who you could never imagine."

Fernando was pacing the room as he listened to Nard. He stopped and lowered his head and tears began to fall. Once he raised his head, his eyes were red, his nose was running and he had a slight smirk on his face.

Nard embraced Fernando and said to him, "What's so funny?"

Fernando pointed to Nard's eye and said, "Your eye Unc. It's a shiner."

Nard pushed Fernando away from him and headed to the mirror. He turned around and said to Fernando, "You know I'm going to get me some get back right?"

AS FERNANDO DROVE down his mom's driveway it brought back memories of his father White. Fernando reminisced on the times when he and father would be in the front yard shooting coke cans with his BB gun. White was the reason that Fernando fell in love with guns. As Fernando got older he graduated from shooting BB guns in the front yard to shooting big guns in the gun range. One thing White always lectured him on was to never surround himself where the enemy has the upper hand, and to choose his battles wisely.

"That was some advice!"Fernando thought to himself.

Tina broke Fernando from his daydreaming.

"J.R.!"she shouted from the front porch, as she gestured for him to come inside.

Fernando hated the way that he zoned out and daydreamed most of the time when he visited the family house.

"There's my baby!"she said.

She was so excited to see him that she almost knocked the bags out of his hands as she hugged on him.

"Dang ma!"Fernando.

"You always do that." he said as he wiped off her kisses. "And you know I got to save some for my other women." Fernando said jokingly.

Tina smacks the back of Fernando's head playfully. "Boy, shut up and come give your sister a hug."

"I might need to try this again because y'all acting way too different,"Fernando said as he turned up his nose.

"Let's go in the living room and sit down because it seems like y'all need to tell me something,"Fernando said.

Monique was the first to blow, telling Fernando how she felt. Tina sat there embarrassed, and didn't say anything, while Monique poured her business out like she was a child. After Monique was done snitching on their mom, silence filled the room. Fernando noticed the frustrating look on his mom's face, and he instantly took offense.

"Ma, like I told Monique yesterday, the only reason she dislikes Alex is because of the amount of money in his bank account. I keep trying to tell her that money don't bring people happiness in a relationship,"Fernando said.

"I show don't see you messing with no broke females,"Monique said sarcastically and then buried her eyes back on her phone.

"That's where you are wrong sis, because you don't see me at all. We ain't seen each other in how long?"Fernando snapped.

Monique got up, and ran off upstairs emotional and in her feelings.

"She'll get over it eventually," Tina whispered. "You know her and Reggie recently broke up. So I've been giving her her space to deal with it the way she needs to."

"Mom. Shoot, I'm surprised it lasted this long. Ain't ole boy some kind of surgeon?"Fernando asked.

"Yes, he works at Grady."Tina responded.

She continued, "Son, I need your honest opinion on something."

"What's up Mom?"Fernando leaned in.

"About a month ago, Alex took me for my monthly check up at Grady. Afterwards we sat and ate in the cafeteria. and J.R. she paused.I saw Reggie hooked up with this white girl,"Tina looked around. I swear, I wanted to run home and tell Monique but she ain't never been this happy with any man so I didn't. Because J. R., your mama loves to see her kids happy."

Fernando shook his head in disappointment and said. "Ma, I really wish you would have just told her, that would have prevented a whole lot of drama. But now ain't the right time to tell her nothing, because ain't no telling what my lil sis might do."

"I hate myself for getting caught up with Alex and neglecting my child."

"Stop talking like that Mom,"Alex continued. You are a grown woman and we are grown, too. You and dad raised us the best way that y'all could, and I can't complain. But like you said, she'll get over it."

Fernando started to unfold his knowledge about what happened to his dad to his mom but he decided against it. Before leaving his mom's house, he started to holla at Monique but decided not to add fuel to the fire. Monique was waiting to hear her brother walk out of the front door and for her mom to go into her room and close the door before she decided to come back out of her room.

Once she noticed that the coast was clear she ran downstairs to get her phone that was left purposely on the loveseat recording the whole conversation. She made it back to her room and played Tina's confession over and over. Her feelings were at a boiling point that tangled between hate and betrayal, and in her heart, she knew the reason Tina held back the news. It was to keep her going, so that she could have Alex all to herself. She grabbed her car keys and headed for the front door with malice in her heart and on her mind.

WHILE GROWING UP, Fernando used to hear his dad brag about how good Mr. Quick was when it came to fixing and rebuilding old school cars. Once Fernando became of age and learned the game, there was no question that he would eventually use Mr. Quick's services. Fernando pulled into Mr. Quick's shop so that he could view his *Mustang*.

"I can't wait to jump into my baby!"Fernando said to himself.

He looked over to his left and spotted a worker polishing up the paint job on his car. His 1965 mustang wore a candy red paint. There was a midsize blower that pierced the hood and a black mustang printed on the back of the trunk.

Mr. Quick waved at Fernando from his office.

He yelled, "Fernando come on in son!"

Fernando headed towards Mr. Quick's office. One step seemed like two as he approached Mr Quick in a hurry.

"It's good to see you son. I saw you checking out some of my babies out there."Mr. Quick said. "Let me find out you are trying to put a project together to put on the track next summer," Mr. Quick continued.

"Naw not yet, but I did see a Monte Carlo with the NASCAR paint job on it just like I like it. It's old but with my money and your time we definitely can make some shake,"Fernando said.

"Sorry son. That one there is for Rich Boy. He bought it last week,"Quick explained. "I'm just waiting on the rest of my funds,"he grinned.

"That baby gone be hurtin em. I gotta step my game up. What do you think?"Fernando asked.

"I don't see why. Come with me and let me show you something,"Mr. Quick said.

Mr. Quick and Fernando walked through the breezeway until they reached the carport.

Mr. Quick unplugged the buffer, the worker looked around wondering what had just happened. Once he realized it was Mr. Quick signaling for him to crank up the vehicle, the worker put the key in ignition and made the 1965 Mustang come alive. The motor roared and was loud and thunderous. Fernando was all smiles as he listened to the engine roar. He sat in the driver's seat, and continued to press the gas.

"Mr Quick, where did you put the nitrogen switch?"

"It's in the console. I can't afford for that to be visible."Mr. Quick said and lowered his head to look over his glasses. "You know what I mean?"

"Damn! I can't wait to hit the road." Fernando said.

He was still pressing the gas.

"You might want to lay off the gas some because of the size of the tank. This monster gone do a lot of gas guzzling."Mr. Quick said to him.

Fernando tossed him the keys to his suv because he wanted to take a test drive.

"Be careful and don't be acting a fool around them dumbass police,"Quick said as he pointed at the *Zone 6* police precinct next door.

"I got you UNC,"said Fernando. "Give me 30 minutes at the most, his eyes read differently."

Fernando backed out from the shop, he put the car in gear and did the opposite of what he was just told not to do. After the smoke cleared from under the tires, he eased up to the fork of the road, looked both ways, then he came off the brake and gave the streets more smoke. Luckily there wasn't a cop in sight, and he didn't even bother stopping at the red light on Howard Street.

Fernando sped west of Hosea Williams Boulevard and headed towards Edgewood. He knew everybody would be hanging in front of the infamous *Red Store* around this time of day, so this was his chance to put on. Fernando made a right hand turn off of Hosea Williams drive on to Mason Avenue getting up to speeds of 70 mph until he reached the four-way stop sign at the *Red Store*. Once he made a right hand turn onto *Hardee Street,* he opened up his exhaust pipes making the mustang scream as loud as it could.

Deon opened the front door wearing an Atlanta Braves fitted cap very low on his head. He scrambled around the apartment after opening the door. Fernando stood there skeptically. At the first sight of seeing Deon, Fernando knew something was wrong.

"Fam you good?" he asked. "And what's up with that big ass hat you're wearing?" Fernando said.

"Bro me and that nigga Rich Boy got into it last night."Deon took off his hat. "It ain't too bad is it?"

Fernando was shocked as he noticed the bruising. "Hell yeah! And what the hell was it all about anyways?"

"That bitch Nicole,"Deon answered.

Fernando threw his hands up. "I already told you bro! But this shit wasn't my fault. Last night this bum ass hoe pulled up while I was smoking outside and asked to hit my weed. I told Shawty to stop trying me. Then she went crazy on my ass, like the shit was pre-planned or something. To make a long story short, Rich Boy heard us arguing and ran up on me. We started hitting. I ain't go out bad either. His lame ass caught me a few times, but I busted bra up real good doe. And I know that nigga gone need some stitches."Deon boasted.

Deon went to the mirror and checked his eye. Through the reflection, he saw the frown Fernando wore.

"I'm good bra. Shawty ain't gone want no smoke,"Deon said

Fernando shook his head in disappointment.

He and Rich Boy did business together, and he knew what the response would be. And that was retaliation.

He damn near had to explain to Deon twice how Rich Boy rock for his safety, and he insisted that he pack a bag and come chill at his spot for a while.

Deon was a little hesitant.

Fernando went into more depth about the consequences.

He complied. They left.

Midway down the steps, there were five unfamiliar faces sitting looking suspicious. Fernando began to feel around his waist and realized that there was no weapon.

"Damn,"he said to himself.

Deon felt a sense of relief when he retrieved his 38 Smith & Wesson. The men instantly rose up with their hands in the air and they began backing up.

"Y'all fools must got a problem,"Deon said.

Deon waved his gun.

"This is private property right here. Y'all got to find some other place to hang out bro."Deon yelled.

"We ain't come for no drama. One of the men said. He continued saying, I'm trying to put you up on game about *Rich Boy*, and all I need you to do is listen for one second. See last night…."

Fernando cut him off by shaking his head from left to right indicating not to say anything, so he handed him a business card.

The dude nodded his head up and down signaling that he understood.

"I'm Cali. That's a bet."

Fernando knew that rich boy was more than likely somewhere watching.

Then the two of them went their separate ways.

Before Fernando reached the interstate, Deon asked him what was so special about the nitrogen tank. He didn't have to ask twice. Fernando told Deon to buckle up. He hit Highway 20 East heading towards Panola Road and stepped on the gas doing the whole speed limit on the dashboard.

"Nando, you got yourself a real machine here. But when you went around that one curve it felt like you almost lost it bra,"Deon said.

"I felt the same thing and that shit almost scared me on the low."Fernando said

They both shared a laugh.

The first place that Fernando stopped was the front office of the storage unit. He updated his plan and pulled out to check on his prize possessions.

"I got to start coming out here more often. This shit collects more cob webs than a mother fucker, Nando said.

This was Deon's first time seeing the different styles of artillery that he kept. There were AR-15s, AK-47s, Machine guns, Mac 10s, grenades and scopes with beams attached. Deon's eyes widened as he looked at all of the heavy artillery that surrounded him.

"You must be trying to go to war with this whole city my nigga. This shit crazy fam!"Deon said as he looked around.

"Empty your tote bag, so I can grab a few things,"Fernando said as he checked the time.

"Damn, I got to make it back to Quick's shop before he closes so we got to speed up,"Fernando said.

"Did you drive the Porsche?"Deon asked Fernando.

"Yeah my nigga, now hurry up so I can get back to Kirkwood."Fernando said.

AFTER FERNANDO SWUNG through Kirkwood to holla at Mr. Quick, Deon followed him over to the infamous ***Ms. Ann's*** hamburger shack to snatch up a couple of her famous ***Ghetto Burgers.***

The diner was quiet as normal. Deon always joked at how *Ms. Ann* had the whole hood shook when you entered her diner. *Ms. Ann* was known for making sure that all of her customers, especially the men, were respectful.

The local police also frequently showed up there as well, so people knew that they couldn't be on the bullshit when they came up in there. Fernando was quiet as a Catholic School kid because he knew that if he made one false move, he was out of there because *Ms. Ann* didn't play. She was known for putting people out of her restaurant without hesitation.

Deon looked Fernando's way and then broke out laughing.

*Ms. Ann* shot him a look as if she wanted to say, "One more time young nigga and you gone."

Deon tightened up so that he didn't get put out.

After 15 minutes, their food was ready and they were gone.

By the time Deon and Fernando made it to Auburn Avenue, Fernando noticed that Deon was done eating and dropping his plate in the trash can.

"Nigga you done?"Fernando shouted.

Deon looked at him with a confused look.

"What?"Deon said, looking embarrassed like a fat kid.

Fernando cracked jokes on Deon all the while they walked up the stairs. When they approached the front door, they noticed a letter attached to it.

It confused Fernando.

It had Nicole's name printed on it. He was more worried about how she had got his address. Seconds later his phone rang and the name Cali appeared on his screen. He took the letter away and decided to read it later.

He answered with a serious tone.

Cali explained everything from square one. Nicole got in touch with her overseers and her father told her to contact them in case of an emergency. But the truth be told, Nasty really put them in position to watch *Rich Boy* more than anything. While *Nasty Red* maintained his position under *El Helzer*, overseeing the smuggling of marijuana from the east to the west coast, he hired a guy named *Cali* and once the call came in from Cali he had to inform his boss about the measures at hand. This was the eye opener for *Nasty Red.* Plus he really wanted to find a reason to get rid of his daughter's boyfriend.

*Cali* gave them the rest of the blueprint, and scheduled a meeting for the next day to finish capitalizing on their scheme because it was all about who gets who first

# CHAPTER 7

## The Truth

MONIQUE SAT IN the parking lot of North Atlanta High School watching and waiting to see if there was any kind of strange activity going on around her ex Reggie's estate. The only movement that she recognized was the gardener doing his job. It was 2:00 p.m. The mailman came and delivered the mail at 2:30 p.m. and a few school kids walked past the house at 3:30 p.m. Monique started to become restless and was about to leave, until she saw a beige Infinity turn into the driveway and park near the front door. She watched as a slender, middle aged redhead stepped out of the driver's side of the vehicle. Monique instantly became sick to stomach.

Reggie opened the door to his home wearing nothing but some boxers with American flags all over them. He greeted his company with a huge hug and kiss. Monique decided to leave, before she decided to do something crazy and things got out of hand. Monique had just seen what she needed to see. The answers to her questions had just been revealed to her right before her eyes, and now she was ready for revenge.

MONIQUE DROVE IN silence thinking. It began to dawn on her that if she wanted to slang dirt and be dirty, the best place to learn how to do that was in the hood, however going to Kirkwood was out of the question because that was her old stomping grounds. Monique chose the westside of Atlanta instead because she wasn't as known. And on Sundays on the Westside over half of the area would be chilling. Not at home, not at the mall, but at *Moseley Park* .

~~~

THE FOLLOWING WEEK…
Sunday…

Monique stepped out of her *Lincoln* SUV, wearing a Chanel bodysuit that complimented her curves just right. She wore a pair of *Jimmy Choo* open toe sandals that showed her pretty manicured toes.

Her feminine swag had all eyes glued to her and her voluptuous booty. One native of the Westside named *Creshon* stared her down and undressed her with his eyes. Monique stared back at him as she sat curbside at the park. She had run into him at the mall two days ago but they didn't speak. However, they both lusted after each other. From the moment that Creshon layed eyes on Monique, he knew that she was everything that her looks displayed. Monique had bougie written all over her. She was an A plus in his eyes.

Creshon approached Monique and said, "Your eyes are beautiful ma."

"Why thank you! I probably get it from my momma,"Monique giggled.

"You can be modest all you want ma, but I know you're one of a kind," Creshon said.

He was crossing every 'T'and dotting all his 'I's'and Monique blushed from ear to ear as he did so.

Creshon's occupation was in moving and flipping cars, just not the kind that came off the lot. They were the ones that traveled throughout the black market. He co-owned a chop shop on Bankhead with his childhood friend named Struggle.

Their establishment was built with money they got from hitting licks. His conversation invaded Monique's ears like no other man's conversation had ever done before. Monique knew that Creshon was well respected in his hood, so that made Monique feel a sense of protection. That day was Creshon's birthday. He invited her to his house on Stanton Road for the party that he was having. Initially Monique was hesitant, but the
~~~

thought of Reggie and his new girlfriend made her realize that there was no way that she would miss this.

LATER THAT NIGHT…

Monique yelled over the music to make sure that she was heard. "Creshon! Why haven't I seen you smoking? If it's because of me I want you to know that I don't mind you smoking because the smoke doesn't bother me because my dad smoked and my brother stays smoking.

"Smoking ain't never been my thing, Moe! I fucks with the drank!"Creshon responded.

"I could sure use me a drink. Because all this smoke got me feeling light-headed."Monique said, coughing slightly. "I believe I done caught a damn contact," she continued.

"My bad for being rude. Follow me,"Creshon said as they pushed through the crowded house, hand in hand. They finally reached the kitchen and it was empty.

"I want some of that,"Monique said as she pointed at the purple punch bowl.

"Do you even know what that is?"he asked.

Monique nodded yes. Creshon gave her one more reassuring look before pouring up two plastic cups. Monique had prepared herself before the party. She had googled and researched about what all goes on at most hood parties? She had never smoked weed before and wasn't about to start, and having dirty urine was a "no no"for her, so she figured that if she drank a little cough syrup it wouldn't do any major damage. Monique was naive. She sipped on the sizurb while Creshon watched her every move. He wasn't new to the drank, and the way she was babysitting her cup, let him know that this was her first time.

**3 Hours later…**

"Say Moe. It's getting late."Creshon said as he tapped her on her shoulder.

"You good Moe?"He asked.

Monique jumped up from her nod in a daze…"Huh huh!"

"I'm not letting you drive home like this. Let me get your keys, come on, I'll take you home,"Creshon said.

"Why can't I stay with you?"Monique slurred.

"That's your choice,"he said. "I was just letting you know that you had options."

"That's so thoughtful…hiccup…of you, but no thanks I'm good right here…hiccup,"Monique pouted looking around and burping.

"Where's everybody?"she asked, standing up. "Did I miss the whole party?"

"Whoa, now!"Creshon said as he grabbed her arm.

Monique caught her balance as Creshon walked her to his bedroom. The party had been over for about 45 minutes.

"I couldn't leave your side. you were asleep,"he told her.

Creshon and Monique made it to his bedroom.

"Awwhhh my head feels like crap!"she told him.

"Lay down and relax and it'll blow over." Creshon told Monique and then walked off.

"Creshon!"Monique called out, "Why you leaving me?" She whined.

"Let me straighten up the living room and kitchen and then I'll be back to join you."

"Do you need my help?"she asked.

"Moe get some rest. I promise I'll be right back and it'll be just me and you chillin for the rest of the night okay?"

*Monique* nodded and then *Creshon* left the room.

"Oooh weee! How in the hell did I luck up like this?"*Creshon* asked himself as he looked around the house for party stragglers. He found Struggle sitting on the porch talking on the phone.

"*Stro*! I thought you had been gone bro!"Creshon said.

*Struggle* held up one finger indicating that he was on an important call. He finally ended the call and said. "Yeah, I was about to leave but business was calling. And shit don't stop for your boy. Shiiit Imma be up all night too. I don't get tired."*Struggle* boasted.

"And who Lil Shawty is who showed up late? Old girl got a fat ass!"

Creshon sat down next to *Struggle* and said, "I've been meaning to scream at you about shawty. So far from what I see she ain't no hood bitch and I can tell her folks got to have a sack because shawty riding in the latest whip and she dripped in designer gear too. During the little time that we have been chopping it up she ain't said nothing about going to no job, so you already know what I'm trying to do wit that! Shiiit come up!"He said as he gave *Struggle* some dap.

"I see her whip still here. Where the hell she at?"*Struggle* asked.

"Shawty tried to drink for the first time and done sipped herself damn near into a coma."*Creshon* said jokingly.

"Nigga you ain't smashed yet?"*Struggle* asked.

*Creshon* gave him a questionable look and said, "Hell naw fool! You must ain't hear what I just said. I said she in there knocked out, off the drank bro! Man your ass is crazy! I aint bout that life!"*Creshon* said in a frustrated tone.

He and *Struggle* sat and conversated for a while longer, and then *Struggle* left once he made a booty call.

MONIQUE WOKE UP the next morning with the worst headache that she'd ever had. She was exactly the way Creshon had left her and that was by herself. She walked down the hallway, and paused as she heard somebody talking loudly. She was curious to see who it was. Creshon was on the phone and he was demanding that one of his workers either pay him or bring him a car for collateral. The bottom line for Creshon was he wanted his money and he didn't care how they got it. She felt nervous in the pit of her stomach, and it was not a good feeling. She went back to the bedroom to gather her things, and with everything in hand she sat quietly in the hallway. She took a deep breath then tried passing him and signaling for him to call her later. He held up his hand and covered the receiver.

"I'll be with you in one minute," he whispered.

He cut his eyes at her and saw the disappointing expression on her face, he figured that it would be best to take the call he was on later. He hung up the phone and put his focus on Monique.

"Okay, now back to you, pretty lady,"Creshon said. "Why are you trying to jet off so fast? You know we ain't had time to talk about anything really sleepyhead."

"Calm down, big baby. I'm here now, so let me hear what you have to say, I'm all ears."Monique said.

"Now that you're good and sober, what made you drink that cup of lean last night? And please don't try to come at me sideways, cuz I already know what's up,"Creshon asked her.

Monique grinned and shook her head.

She said, "You think you know me huh?"

"Monique, I've been sipping syrup for a while now. And I know how it affected me the first time I tried it,"he said.

"Creshon look, I'm going to be straight up with you. I just went through a hard break up and I've been stressed. My lame ass ex started cheating on me with this white girl. Ever since I found out, I've been doing things that are out of my character such as this. Truthfully I ain't never done anything illegal in my whole life,"Monique said.

"I know, I can tell,"Creshon said.

"Please don't judge me."Monique said.

She lowered her head and continued. "The reason I came out to the park was to find someone to help me make my ex feel some of the fucked up feeling that I've been feeling."

Creshon sat straight up and gave Monique his full attention.

"What you had in mind Moe?"

"I don't know. I'm not an expert in doing stuff like this. I was hoping you could maybe come up with something." Monique said.

"Are you hungry? "Creshon asked

Monique nodded her head, signaling yes.

Creshon responded, "All right. Let's go grab a bite to eat then we'll think of something because I'm starving."

# CHAPTER 8

## In and Out

"What time does *Cali* want us to be there?"Fernando asked as he checked his watch.

"We got like an hour. Why what's up?"

"I got some people on the southside trying to spend 10 bandz on a bag. Do you got em on deck?"Deon asked.

"Yeah! Fuck yeah I got em! For 10 bandz…you should have been said something. Let me put my folks on standby, then we can dip!"Fernando said with excitement.

"Bet!"Deon responded.

Fernando gathered everything that he needed before reweighing the pound of weed.

"Good business brings future customers,"he thought to himself before they left.

HAVING TO RESORT back to his old ways, *Alex* reached out to one of his old running mates because hustling was all they knew. At age 60, *Calvin* was still doing his thing. *Calvin* was an OG in the game. He sold plenty of weed, but he had changed up how he and Alex used to do it. Calvin and Alex used to take trips to the West Coast. In the beginning, they were just traveling to the west coast in the blind. They would get there and mingle around for weeks at a time trying to find a new plug.

EVENTUALLY, THEY STUMBLED upon someone that heard their plea for a new plug. The new plug sold them 50 pounds of high grade weed at $1,000 a pound. They thought to themselves that hard work pays off. But now things were different and times had changed. Because he was about to pay $10,000 dollars for one pound, and it didn't make any sense to him or make him feel good about paying that amount of money for a pound. Alex kept trying to calculate in his head how he was going to make a profit. He was stuck. The bourbon they sipped had his mind going in a whole new direction.

"Excuse me for one second. I got to take a leak,"Alex said as he left the garage.

Calvin had his eyes glued to the road as he waited on the delivery.

"I can do this,"Alex repeated to himself as he splashed water on his forehead.

He looked down then lifted his pants leg up to retrieve a 380.

"Alex!"Calvin shouted. "My people just pulled up!"

He waited for a minute so whoever it was would be waiting for his surprise.

"DEON. ARE YOUR folks straight? Cuz that's a lot of cake to be spending on one bag." Fernando asked.

"Yeah it's one of my personal customers, you know how I roll. I don't really serve them fools in the apartment. I tried my best to get most of my money outside the hood,"Deon replied.

"Well here you go. "Fernando said. "Imma let you handle everything."

Deon put the YSL bookbag on his shoulder, and took off.

**20 Minutes later…**

TIME SEEMED LIKE it was moving fast. Fernando checked his watch.

"What the hell Deon got going on?"He thought to himself.

Since Deon was taking so long to respond, Fernando tried calling him. Deon's phone started vibrating on the front seat of his car. Fernando hung up when Deon didn't answer. And now Fernando had to see what was going on.

~~~

"ALEX! DAMN IT man why won't you listen?" Calvin pleaded

"I'm going to tell you one more time, shut up!"Alex shouted

Alex was obviously nervous from the way the sweat ran down his forehead. He was also shaking really bad as he waved the gun.

"Don't worry. Your little friend is going to be just fine." Alex said.

"BOOM! BOOM! BOOM! BOOM!"Someone was beating on the front door, and Alex's blood was pumping.

"Keep them hands up!"Alex yelled.

He knew it was now or never, so Alex grabbed the book bag and fled out the back door. As soon as the back door slammed, Deon jumped up and ran towards the front door and opened it. When Deon finally opened the door, immediately, Fernando sensed that there was a problem. Both of them looked at each other and had a baffled expression on their faces.

"YOU MIGHT WANT to sit down for this one bra."Deon said.

Fernando sat down and listened to the rundown of what had just happened. Based on what he was hearing he felt like the situation and information seemed flakey. Fernando shook his head at the carelessness of the transaction.

"Do anybody know where this guy lives or possibly went to?"Fernando asked as he stared Calvin down with a stern look.

"This shit all bad. I should have known better. Fuck! How in the hell did I let this nigga catch me down bad like that?"Deon shouted.

He looked at Calvin and said, "I thought you was the one trying to get the shit! That's bad business bro. You should have told me that somebody else was in on the play. I don't get down like that old school."

"This shit took me by surprise, too! I didn't think that nigga would pull a stunt like that!"Calvin said as he shook his head in discus. "It never crossed my mind, but I'm going to straighten everything out on my end with the money. I got you. Trust me."
~~~

"I know damn well you do, cuz if you ask me old man I think you was in cahoots with this shit."Fernando said, looking dead serious.

"Deon, tell your friend that I don't get down like that. I ain't got to take nothing from nobody,"Calvin said, looking at Deon.

"WELL, IF THAT'S your partner, you got to know his name and where he lives right?"Fernando asked.

Deon stayed calm and focused so that he could see if Calvin was about to start lying.

"His name is Alex Monroe and he lived right across from the *College Park* train station."Calvin explained.

"Do you know the name of the apartments?"Fernando asked.

"I think they're called *College Park Heights,*"Deon said.

Fernando grew angry upon hearing the name of the robber.

He asked, "Was he plotting to rob the house or me?"

He rushed to the door without saying a word or waiting for a response. Deon pocketed the money from Calvin and ran to catch up with Fernando before he pulled off. Deon jumped in the car. They both sat in silence until Deon asked Fernando,

"Aye bro, the look you just gave me back there made it seem like dude's name sounded familiar?"

Fernando bangs on the steering wheel.

"You ain't going to believe this shit bro,"Fernando yelled.

His face showed more malice than ever before.

"Calm down and let me know what's going on bro."

"Man! Alex was my mom's personal driver until Monique caught the two of them in the bed,"Fernando said.

"We got the info. And he ain't going to be hard to find. But on the flip side we got the money. We could just let it go Fernando. We ain't got to send that nigga through the flame! He ain't got to feel the heat from this smoke pole,"Deon said.

"Fuck that Deon! That nigger tried my family and me bro. I took up for that nigga when Moe spazzed out on me about him. And now I feel lame as hell."Fernando yelled.

Time was ticking, and Fernando knew it.

"Call Cali and let bro know we're on the way,"Fernando said to Deon.

Deon texted hs partna *Hollywood* to see if he was down to pull-up and slide through on this nigga.

CALI AND HIS boys were waiting in the parking lot of the train station. It was fairly empty as Fernando scanned the surrounding areas. He spotted a white Tahoe and white Crown Vic that both had tinted windows. Cali exited the truck wearing a fitted black ATF shirt with a fake badge hanging from his neck. The rest of the crew followed suit with similar gear.

Nichole needed to be out of the way, and *Nasty Red* informed the crew that not a hair on Nichole's head was to be touched. Fernando had to think fast. He placed the call and invited her out to eat, so that she wouldn't be anywhere near the scene.

The sky darkened as time ticked down on the clock. Deon picked up his walkie-talkie and said, "0-4."

"0-4" was the code to let them know that everything was clear enough for them to proceed. Cali and his goons pulled off. Fernando and Deon fell back and waited until the enemy was captured and brought to them.

The Tahoe made a round through the apartments just to make sure that everything was safe. Once the coast was clear, the Tahoe parked next to the black Camero behind the target across from the apartment complex.

"Green light fellas,"Cali said over the walkie-talkie.

They all pulled down their masks over their faces and exited the vehicles moving in full pursuit of the target.

BOOM was the sound that was heard when *Rich Boy's* door came crashing down . They kicked in the door as if it was a no knock arrest warrant procedure.

"Whoa! Whoa!"*Rich Boy* said as he was caught by surprise.

They came through the front and back door. The pyrex pot he had shattered when it hit the floor.

"Shit!"Were the last words that came out of *Rich Boy's* mouth.

Rich Boy had never experienced a level of fear like this before. He had found himself in tight situations, but not like this one. Most times, he had always managed to dodge or get himself out of the situation. Sure, there were repercussions for the risk that he took in the game, but those were supposed to come later, after the fact, when the danger had long passed. This was different; and from the looks of things, these men intended to kill him.

He thought to himself for a second, "Are these real police?"

He doubted it. But he knew that if he continued to resist, whoever they were might just shoot him right then and there. So he gave the gun that was jammed into his gut the respect that it deserved. When they sensed that Rich Boy was co-operating they told him to walk.

"Stand up straight nigga!"One of the men ordered.

He lowered his head and got into the back seat of the car. He kept a watchful eye on the gun that was aimed at him. The Crown Vic eased from the curb and exited the apartment complex.

"Be patient,"he told himself. He was hoping that there was a way out of this. "Wait for an opportunity," he thought to himself. "But when? Where? How?"

And from the looks of things, the prospect didn't seem promising.

Cali radioed Fernando. "Time to move."

THE HILL STREET exit was their next destination and the *Summer Hill Community* is where they landed. When they got three blocks away from the intended destination, they blind folded *Rich Boy*. They entered through the main door and locked the latch behind them. A staircase was visible at the end of a short hallway. The basement was cold and had huge stone walls everywhere. Two individual light bugs hung from the low ceiling. There was an iron slab in the middle of the floor across from the base of the stairs. They tossed Rich Boy on the floor and he laid there trembling, on the cold steel.

"I see this fool is still alive,"one man said.

"Watch him while I go and help the other two get here. Cali glided up the squeaky stairs. The upper house was empty. When he got to the top of the stairs he made the call.

**Ten minutes later….**

DEON AND FERNANDO pulled up, got out of the car and looked around. There was no grass, no neighbors, no nothing, it was a true *Bando.* They followed Cali's lead down into the basement. Deon knew that when he saw his target, it was on site for him. So he took advantage of the opportunity to handle his business. He grabbed an empty liquor bottle and swung it across Rich Boy's face. It crashed on his temple and blood was everywhere.

"Awwwwh!"Rich Boy yelled in agony.

Deon ripped the duct tape off his mouth, and said, "What up soft ass nigga?"

Deon spit in Rich Boy's face.

"That new look fits you!"He said as he landed a punch to Rich Boy's eye.

Fernando grabbed Deon's shoulder, and whispered, "I don't think we need to get carried away. Let Cali finish this. I see how this is going to turn out,"Deon nodded in agreement and said, "Mission accomplished."

# CHAPTER 9

## Shadow of Death

*Hollywood's* street cred earned him instant respect in the hood. At first, he thought of himself as a knight or a rook on the chessboard. However, he now carried the distinct feeling of being the King on the chess board. *Hollywood* was a well known figure in *Atlanta.* He was flashy and a show off, but most of all he was a straight up killer from the *Thomasville Heights* apartments in Zone 3.

When he and *Fernando* first met, it was at the *Foxy Lady* strip club. Their initial meeting didn't get off on the right foot because when *Hollywood* approached *Fernando* trying to sell some jewelry, *Fernando* took it the wrong way thinking *Hollywood* was trying to check his pockets and rob him. *Fernando* had been drinking alot and the liquor had begun to have an impact on his thinking.

*Deon* eventually was able to calm the situation between the two of them by telling *Fernando* to chill because *Hollywood* wasn't a threat. The liquor had been talking for *Fernando* and he didn't hold back.

And as the saying goes "When a drunk man is talking, you better listen because he is spilling his truth."

After Deon reassured *Fernando* that everything was cool and that Hollywood was just trying to make some money by selling his products, *Fernando* invited him up to the V.I.P to smoke. When *Hollywood* entered the V.I.P area, they both fired up a blunt that was provided by *Fernando.* Each one of them took turns joking around and making fun about their first encounter. Fernando eventually found out that the jewelry that *Hollywood* was selling was A-1 and official. That made *Fernando* decide to begin collaborating with *Hollywood* on a few other business deals.

Three months into their business dealings, and plenty of lucrative business transactions later, Fernando felt comfortable enough with meeting *Hollywood* whenever and wherever he wanted him too, even if it was outside of his comfort area which was *Zone 6*. *Fernando's* level of trust with *Hollywood* had increased and today their current meeting spot was on *Custard Avenue* at the pool hall. *Hollywood* had a *Presidential Rolex* with a diamond bezel that he wanted to sell, and *Hollywood* knew that with one call to Fernando, it would be taken off of his hands and gone asap.

While *Hollywood* was showing *Fernando* the watch, some dude came running out of the pool hall with his pistol aimed at the two of them demanding that they give up the watch and their money.

"You know what it is! Give me that shit nigga! Lay it down!"The robber said.

He hesitated busting his gun and pulling the trigger. But *Hollywood* didn't, he opened fire immediately in response to the threat that was before him.

Pop! Pop! Pop! Pop! The sound of the gun was all anyone heard.

*Hollywood* emptied the clip on the robber in broad daylight. Blood splattered everywhere and the unknown assailant, in his after life, wished that he could have lived another day to make a better decision.

That experience was the beginning of a bond that was fostered between Fernando and Hollywood that would be hard for anyone to come between. It created a dynamic chemistry between the two of them. In *Fernando's* mind, he knew that there would be a time when *Hollywood's* services would come in handy. And the situation with *Rich Boy* was the perfect one to start with….

~~~
~~~

*HOLLYWOOD* WAS ON Moreland Avenue in his stomping grounds when he received the text message. He left the dice game as soon as he received it. *Hollywood* researched the area, and made sure that he knew everything that he needed to know in order to execute the job effectively. Now all he needed was the green light to move forward. *Hollywood* loved to make his moves in the streets. It was as if he was pushing pawns on the chessboard. One thing for sure was whenever it was time for him to make his move, he always checkedmated his opponent.

His phone rang, "Ring, Ring, Da Da Ling!"

"Hello."

"Aye bro, I need you to meet me at my spot. I needed you to be there like an hour ago and I got you bro."Fernando said.

"Say no mo! I am on the move now,"Hollywood responded.

THE *AUBURN AVENUE* festival was filled with people from many different states. The out of towners were enjoying every bit of the festivities in the streets. Most of the residents in the *Cotton Mills Lofts* were sprawled out on the front lawn as they enjoyed the view. Fernando and Deon waited in the parking lot until Hollywood pulled up moments later. Fernando rolled down his window and waved his hand in the direction of Hollywood.

He yelled, "Hey Hollywood! Right here fool!"

Hollywood gave them a head nod and then they both parked. There were females everywhere, but now wasn't the time to be distracted by a pretty face and a fat ass. By the time Hollywood parked, Fernando and Deon were already out of the car walking. Hollywood had to bite his tongue while passing so many beautiful women.

The elevator ride was quiet. It ain't no telling who was watching, or listening. Once they were inside of Fernando's apartment Deon was the first to break the silence.

"Nando, did you ever get around to reading that letter from Nichole?"

Fernando shook his head in disbelief and said, "Damn bro, I tried forgetting that shit! But that letter was on another planet for real though!"

Deon and Hollywood wanted to know what was so special about the letter.

"We will talk about it later bro. We got shit that we need to be handling right now."Fernando said as he walked towards the kitchen. He hit the lights and said, "Y'all niggas hungry?"

"Nah I'm good. But I'm geeked about the move!"Hollywood said.

"Deon looked up and said to Fernando, "Fuck with me on a few of dem shrimp cocktails! Man them bitches was bussin yesterday."

"I got you fam. Aye Deon, while I'm doing this, can you snatch up that bag on my bed?"Fernando said.

Deon got up and went to the bedroom to get the bag.

Hollywood waited on Deon to come back with the bag. After getting the bag Deon dumped everything out on the sofa.

"Damn bro!"Hollywood said.

He couldn't believe his eyes.

"You must have been shopping at the same place T.I. bought his shit from?"

They laughed.

"Boy you are a fool,"said Fernando. "But on the real, everything is yours. Plus you get five racks to go with it. How does that sound for the job?"

"Shiiiiit. Ole boy is done. I'mma cook his ass fo sho! I am thinking about sliding tonight."Hollywood said and zipped the bag up and then slung it over his shoulder.

Deon counted out five bands and handed Hollywood his fee. Hollywood grabbed the money and thanked Fernando and then left. His next stop was the Southside.

THERE WASN'T MUCH movement on the Southside except for a few hustlers shooting dice. Hollywood reclined in his seat and put on his night vision goggles. He scanned the area. It was dark and the train station parking lot had a great view of the target. He began to grow impatient so he took off.

The dice game had just started and by the looks of the dudes that were playing were only kids. He could have strong armed the young bulls without even pulling a pistol on them, but he decided against it.

"What up fellas? Yall got room for one more?"Hollywood asked.

"Naw not really, but if we let you get in the game you got to catch a fade,"one of the young dudes said.

Hollywood agreed and he began to shoot the dice. When the street lights came on, Hollywood looked up and noticed that the lights in Alex's front room came on as well. Hollywood dropped the dice on the concrete. He turned and looked away one more time at Alex's house. When he picked up the dice this time, he noticed that they felt different. He could tell that the dice had been switched.

He thought to himself as he caressed the dice, "These young niggas don't know who they fucking with!"

Hollywood snatched up the whole pot of money. As he was grabbing the money, he showed the youngins his Ruger, that was attached to his hip.

"Y'all lil bastards must be ready to die because I'm bout ready to let my bitch air out this bitch!"

The kids were scared to death. He shoved his gun into the side of one of the kids belly and said, "Now get the fuck out of here lil niggas!"

The young bulls ran off and left Hollywood standing there with the loot. After the strong arm robbery, Hollywood headed to Alex's house and stood at his door with a *Georgia Power* uniform and hat that was pulled down to the bridge of his eyebrows. He was in full disguise.

"Knock! Knock! Knock!"

The front curtains opened and then they closed really fast. Then Alex made his way to his front door and opened it to greet Hollywood.

"How are you doing this evening sir? I'm from the *Georgia Power* Light Company and I was sent out to give you this notice of an unpaid bill. Also sir your building is pulling and draining a lot of power from your meter and I need to check it to see what the issue is,"Hollywood said as he pulled his hat down a little further to disguise himself.

"Okay but if you don't mind, I was hoping that you can make this quick because *the Hawks* are playing tonight,"Alex said.

Alex gave Hollywood a tired look as he let him into the living room. Hollywood set his work bag on the floor. Alex was still trying to explain to him about the unpaid bill. But Hollywood really didn't give a fuck so he was ignoring him. For a moment, silence filled the air. Then without hesitation Hollywood swiftly removed his gun from his work bag and shoved it into Alex's face. Alex was shocked, and Hollywood didn't waste no time. He didn't talk or play, it was strictly business. Instantly, two shots rang out and two holes were plastered in Alex's forehead. Once Alex was dead on the floor, Hollywood went through the house and took everything that he could that was of value. He lowered his hat, walked back up the hill and once he reached his vehicle he popped the trunk and threw his belongings inside. He hopped in his ride and fled the Southside headed back to Zone 3.

# CHAPTER 10

## What The Lick Reads...

CRESHON WENT OVER a few ideas with Monique as she sat there and listened. Some of the things he said made her very uncomfortable, and that was the reason she held out from disclosing Reggie's address.

They finally came to an agreement about what to do and that was to confiscate Reggie's car, and that was it. So she thought. In her mind she thought to herself the insurance company would replace everything."She kept telling herself.

STRUGGLE AND CRESHON drove to Northside Drive in the tow truck that they would use to snatch Reggie's car like he and Monique discussed. Creshon was geeked up about the lick!

He asked Struggle, "What else do you think we should get bro?"

Struggle responded saying, "Shiiiiit bro we gone see what else that nigga got that's worth taking!"

"Aight bet!" Creshon said.

When they got to Reggies spot they took more than just the car. They decided to take any and everything they thought was of value and they didn't stop there. They had another plan which was to hit Monique's mom's house.

Struggle wore a camouflaged hoodie with a ski mask rolled down over his face. His outfit made him blend into the darkness of the night. He stopped for a moment to re-check the map that Monique drew up for him. Once he got his bearings together he hopped the fence, and was now in Reggie's wooded backyard.

Creshon waited in the school's parking lot.

Struggle eventually spotted the shed that was on the house. "Bingo!"Struggle said to himself while putting his finger on the 'X' on the map. Monique told them that the doors to Reggie's house always stayed open. Once Struggle reached the door, he looked up and was in awe. He thought to himself, "Damn this fool got a big ass house!"

CRESHON SAT IN the car looking like he was nervous, tapping his foot, and checking his watch. From the looks of it, everything was running on schedule. "Oh shit!"He said to himself as he ducked down inside the tow truck trying to avoid making eye contact with an Atlanta Police squad car that was slowly riding by patrolling the area. Creshon grabbed his Smith & Western. The cop shined his squad car's spotlight but he kept on cruising. After the light disappeared, Creshon peeked to see if the cop was gone. Once the cop was gone, Creshon felt his heart drop to the pit of his stomach. He knew that was a sign to let him know that it was better that Struggle was on the inside of the house and not him, at least that's what he told himself.

STRUGGLE LAID ON the floor in the laundry room. He hid behind the double stack washer and dryer. Out of nowhere, Reggie appeared in the kitchen dancing and wearing a pair of red speedo's. The sound of Frank Ocean pumped through the speakers. Struggle shook off his first thought of whether Reggie was pitching to the other side. Struggle slid across the floor, and when Reggie turned around, he dropped the wine glass that he had in his hand as he stared down a long gun barrel.

"What is this all about?"Reggie demanded. Before another word was mouthed, a punch came crashing to his face, sending him falling on his side.

"Who else is here with you?" Struggle yelled.

Reggie held his bloody mouth, and shook his head rapidly from left to right.

"Alright now. If you're lying, shit gone start getting real bloody in this bitch…You understand?" Struggle said with force.

Reggie nodded, and said, "I-I-I…."

"Shut the fuck up! Get up and take me to that safe nigga! And if for one second you think I'm playing, I'ma show yo bitch ass I ain't!"Struggle yelled and shoved his gun into Reggie's gut. "Now play pussy and get fucked!" Struggle followed Reggie towards the steps. "Hurry up Nigga you think I got all day?"

Reggie's hand shook nervously as he opened the safe.

"Damn it man! You got me fucking nervous dude…. Aghh!"Reggie cried out. "Now that was uncalled for. Reggie said,"as he rubbed the back of his head.

Reggie finally opened the safe and Struggle began to remove everything from it. He took all of Reggie's money, jewelry, and checks. The doorbell rang and it surprised Struggle. He paused for a minute to think and then he shoved the gun into the back of Reggie's head and directed him down the stairs.

"Why you ain't tell me you was having company- huh?" Struggle said as he walked and talked with a whisper. "Now it's about to get real interesting." Struggle said mischievously.

He nudged Reggie, and Reggie jumped.

"Look at me!"

Reggie turned around and looked at Struggle as he said, "Answer the door. But remember I got your life in the palm of my hand. And if you try anything funny, I'm blasting yo ass and whoever's on the other side of this door. Reggie nodded his head as if understood, because he knew Struggle wasn't playing.

Reggie peeked out of the door and saw that it was his girlfriend Meghan. He unlatched each lock and she entered along with Creshon close on her heels with a gun at her lower back.

"You showed up just in time. And what's your name snow bunny?"Asked Struggle.

"M-M-M-Megan!" She said in between cries.

"Please don't hurt me. I swear if you let me go, I promise I wont say a word!"She pleaded.

"Bitch shut up!"Creshon said and pushed her towards the steps.

Upstairs, Creshon tied Reggie's hands and feet with the sheets of the bed, while Hollywood ripped Megan's blouse off and began tying her up also..

"How about I show you how a real black man tamed some white pussy!"Struggle said. He had zoned out, almost to the point of losing his cool.

"Don't hurt me please," she cried. I haven't done anything to you. Whatever Reggie has done, that's on him. Can you please just let me go?!"Megan pleaded loudly.

Creshon sensed that Struggle was about to lose his damn mind and do something crazy, so he yelled, "Yo Fall back bra!"

Creshon shot him a look and said, "Grab this shit and let's bounce. We have been here to long as it is."

"Some other time sweet heart. Struggle said as he looked at Megan and kissed her cheek.

"Oh yeah…Playboy. Up them car keys too,"Creshon said.

They jumped in Reggie's ride and as they were pulling out of the driveway, a police squad car was parked behind the tow truck with its lights flashing.

"It's probably the same police officer,"Creshon said.

Creshon made a right on Northside drive. "Damn fam. That was close,"he exhaled heavily. "I'm glad my mind led me in the right direction."He looked at Struggle, "But yo ass needs some help bro."

"I can't help it and I ain't gone lie! Straight up, I love them white girls. But if you're thinking what I think you're thinking naw bra I don't get down like that!"

"Un huh."Creshon said, unsure.

He hit the gas as he approached the highway. The next stop was the chop shop.

# CHAPTER 11

## First Site…

"Hello,"Monique answered.

"Sup Moe, I was calling to tell you that everything went smoothly last night. So what's up? Can I pull up on you or what?"Creshon said.

"You must be a mind reader. I was just sitting here thinking about you boy. My brother and my mom just left, so if you really miss me you better hurry up,"Monique said.

"I'm on my way baby…. Aye Moe."He quickly called out.

"Yes I'm here."Monique said.

"I messed around and deleted your address by mistake. Text it to me real quick."Creshon said

"Okay bye."

The phone went silent.

CRESHON PARKED NEXT to Monique's SUV. As he exited the vehicle he was checking out their spacious yard.

"Damn this bitch is loaded."He said to himself.

He made his way to the estates entrance. At the same time he noticed Monique's shadow as it was getting closer and approaching the front door. The door swung open, and Monique stood there smiling from ear to ear, dressed in her long T- Shirt that read Lick Me.

"How are you today sexy?"He grabbed her hand and spun her around.

"I'm great. How about yourself?"Monique responded.

"I'm better. Are you gonna invite me in or are we gonna sit here and chop it up on the porch?"Creshon said.

"Come on in silly."Monique said.

He looked around in awe of the home's decor as he entered and followed Monique through the house.

"I can tell you had your hands in the decorating of this place."Creshon said.

They approached her bedroom and she opened the door.

"And this room has your name written all over it,"he said.

"Boy please! This room is about to be a thing of the past. I'm in the process of finding my own place, but thank you,"she said.

"Oh Yeah? Well come here sexy girl and let me make you part of my future,"he said and made his move.

The way her T- Shirt hugged her curves, let him know there was nothing under it. No bra, or panties so he knew she was ready to be dicked down.

He slid behind her and began massaging her shoulders.

"Why you feel so tense girl? Am I making you nervous?"He asked while caressing her shoulders.

"No it's your hands, they are so strong and I feel like I am about to melt. Ooooh yes. That feels wonderful,"she said.

After hearing that Creshon clinched a tighter grip and began to massage her deeper.

Monique felt like she was about to lose control as chills went down her spine.

"Let me lay on my stomach."Monique said.

She layed down and then rolled over slowly giving Creshon a full view of her clean shaved pussy. He slid her shirt over her head. Afterwards, he ran his tongue from her shoulders down to the crack of her ass and he didn't stop there, the pussy was the next stop.

"Ummmm Um! Ooooh yes!"She moaned, as her fluids began to run down her thighs.

Creshon tried his best to catch her drips.

Monique was feeling things that no man had ever made her feel. She ran her hands through his hair. Her legs were shaking while she squirmed and tried to run from the tight grip that he had on her. He rolled her over on her back and then ate her pussy as he stroked her asshole with two fingers.

The sexual session was intense but what she felt was relaxed.

She was ready for part two.

His mustache and beard was white from all of the cum that ooozed from her insides. Her thighs were soak and wet as she laid there in ecstasy.

Creshon slapped Monique's clitoris with his dick, she responded by jumping because she was ready to climax again.

"Why are you doing me like this?"She said, breathing heavily. "I need you. Please. Give me that dick!"

Her pussy was tight. So Creshon slowly guided his dick inside of her. Monique's eyes rolled to the back of her head as he entered her walls. She wanted to run but It felt so good that it made her stay right where she was. After three long strokes, his dick was creamy white. He pulled his dick out and watched her pussy throb. He put his tongue back on her wet pussy. She couldn't take the way that his tongue worked. She tried to push back from his grip.

She shook her head with a smile and said, "Boy you too much."

Monique crawled towards Creshon seductively and asked him to lay on his back. Then she stood over him and mounted his manhood as if she was about to ride a horse. Monique began the ride fast not slow, cowgirl style. She bounced up and down with no hands, and never took her eyes off of him.

"How does this pussy feel, baby?" She asked. "Tell me it's good. Tell me it's good!"She repeated. My pussy feels good.. Now tell me who pussy this is. Creshon met her every thrust. "Huh? Tell me! Creshon! Oh! Oh! Baby I'm cumming! Aaaaaah! Yeeess!"She screamed.

He didn't bother pulling out. It was all about her. Creshon was still hard, but wasn't worried about busting his nut, because he had a different motive. Monique laid on his chest. He slipped out of her pussy but Monique reached behind her and put his rock hard dick back in.

He grabbed her face letting her taste her own juices.

Monique slowly rocked back and forth on his dick.

A few minutes later a voice rang out.

"Hey! Monique!"Tina called out. "Whoever's car that is out front, is blocking the garage."

"Oh shit! Cheshon you got to hurry up and put some clothes on,"Monique said as she jumped up really fast.

"Whoa! Whoa! Baby slow down,"he chuckled. "The doors lock right?"Creshon asked.

She nodded yes.

"I'm tripping," she said embarrassed, but that was an understatement. "I guess you can tell that I don't have company often."

"Aye sis!"Fernando knocked and called out. "Open up real quick. Let me show you what I picked up for you."

Knock! Knock! Knock!

"One second J.R...Give me a minute. I'm putting some clothes on,"Monique said.

Fernando went back down stairs to wait for her. Monique rushed to put some clothes on and Creshon sat there still laughing at her.

"How do I look? Is my hair ok?"She rambled.

"Baby you're fine. Except for the glow,"Creshon said jokingly.

"Glow?" Monique responded curiously.

"Yeah. The one you get when you just got the best fuck of your life,"he grinned.

She straddled his lap planting kisses all over his face, and said. "Thank you baby."

Once they were put together, her and Creshon walked down the stairs hand to hand. When Tina and Fernando saw them walking down the stairs, they were shocked as Monique introduced Creshon.

"Mom. J.R. This is Creshon."

Tina gave a dry grin, Fernando only nodded.

"I'ma call you later,"said Creshon. He leaned to her ear and whispered."And try to snap your folks out of their trance. "Then he gave her a wet kiss before leaving out of the door.

"Who was that? I ain't never seen him in the hood,"Fernando asked.

"I ain't never said he was from the hood,"Monique snapped.

"But if you must know, he owns a car dealership in the Westside,"she lied.

"So when did fucking wit street niggas become your thing? And miss me with the sharades Moe, you know I am smarter than a fifth grader."said Fernando.

She knew her brother wasn't slow.

"J.R."she whined. "Why are you talking to me like I'm twelve huh?"She got louder. "I'm grown and I can date who I please because the last time I checked my dad was in the graveyard."

Fernando threw his hands up in defense before walking off. Monique gave her mom a look like I wish you would say some. Tina felt the tension rising and she was next to walk off.

# CHAPTER 12

## I Seen This Somewhere...

IT WAS TWO in the morning. Fernando and Tina were still up talking. After they finally finished talking he smoked a blunt and ended up laying up in his old bedroom where he dozed off. Hearing the shower running woke him up. He jumped up to check and see who would be using the shower at this time of the hour.

"What the fuck! Why are you here, and with my sister?"He said and waited for an answer.

"J.R.!" Monique screamed.

"Do you mind giving me and Deon some privacy?"She said in a calmer tone.

"Bitch!"Fernando caught himself then he turned to walk off then felt a sharp pain pierce his back.

Fernando jumped up, sweating beads on his forehead and chest. That dream seemed so real, he thought, as he rubbed the lower part of his back. The clock read, 6:00 a.m. The scent from the weed in his pocket led him to a box of blunts. He rolled up the blunt before hitting the weight room.

"Are you alright?"He nodded between reps.

"I couldn't sleep either."Tina implied.

He placed the weight bar back on the stand and sat his blunt back in the ashtray.

"Mom. I just had one of the weirdest dreams ever."Fernando and

Tina sat down.

My dream was about my homie Deon and Monique were in the shower and then somebody stabbed me in my back as I was leaving…That's crazy, ain't it huh?"Fernando said.

"Baby, you're just worried about your sister, that's all. She's going to be fine, though,"Tina added calmly.

"I hope so,"Fernando said.

"And don't leave before I fix your favorite breakfast for you,"Tina said.

"You know I can't pass up them biscuits,"he said, then returned his attention back to lifting the weights.

CRESHON LAID IN the shadows as Fernando backed out of the driveway. He smiled at seeing the Mustang.

"That's a check right there!"Creshon said to himself as he thought about snatching it up and taking it to the chopshop.

Fernando busted a right on Clairmont. Creshon pulled out from an empty house two doors down. He tailed him and kept one car between them. The Ford Mustang's motor roared and sounded like it could speed up and get lost at any moment. Fernando purposely switched lanes twice to see if anyone was following him and if everything he was thinking and feeling was adding up. And from the looks of it so far it was all adding up.

Creshon maneuvered in and out of lanes behind the cars still trying to keep up.

"I see somebody want some smoke,"Fernando said and began scrolling through his phone contacts.

He hit the call button once he reached Hollywood's number. The phone rang twice and then Hollywood answered the phone.

"Hollywood! Wake you black as up! You ever heard the old saying? Sleep late loose cake?"Fernando said jokingly.

"Yeah I heard that shit befoe! What up Foolio? What up doe?"Hollywood responded.

"Shid…I'm just trying to see if you down for a putting a lil work this morning."Fernando said.

"I'm always ready,"Hollywood said.

"Aight bet! I got this fool that's been following me since I left mom dukes. I'm trying to see how bad whoever he or she is want it."Fernando explained.

"Don't worry big bra, I damn sho got it for em."Hollywood responded. "I am out the door right now. Meet me at the strip club on Moreland by my apartments and I'll handle the rest."

"What time the spot open?" Fernando asked nervously.

"We got a good two hours. We Gucci my dude,"Hollywood said.

"Say no mo then!"Fernando said and then ended the call.

He slowed down driving. At the time, he was driving through Decatur. He noticed that his follower had fallen three cars behind, while trying to be incognito and conceal their identity. So they thought. Ten minutes later, he was parking in the parking lot of the Foxy Lady.

Hollywood wasn't anywhere in sight. Fernando got out, and pretended to be on the phone. The car with the tinted windows turned into the parking lot of the yellow corner store that sat across the street. Instantly, Hollywood walked from behind the club wearing a black hoodie and a black New York Giants fitted hat as he scanned the area. Fernando gave him a nod, letting him know that it was only one car at the store.

Hollywood staggered across the street while pulling his cap down at the same time. He looked like a bomb on the street. He walked up and said, "Hey say homie! Say homie!"

He motioned for the driver to let down his window.

Creshon was agitated. And in his mind he thought to himself, "Another damn homeless drunk!"

He rolled down his window and said, "What up my nigga? I ain't got no mother fucking spare cigga..."

Pop! Pop! Pop!

Three shots went through the driver side door and went straight through Creshon's body. He was left slumped over the steering wheel. Hollywood calmly walked off through the shadows and into the cut. Gone in 60 seconds, and job well done. Fernando put his car in reverse out onto Moreland Ave and then he jammed it into drive and sped off south towards highway 285 with a clear view.

"ANSWER THE DOOR!" Monique, I'm in the shower!"Tina yelled from the bathroom.

"I swear I'm tired of this lady,"Monique said to herself aggravated as she walked to the front door of their home.

Monique got to the door and she paused when her vision became visible. She noticed that it was two officers.

"What do they want?"she asked herself. "May I help you?"Monique asked the officers through the door.

"Maam, we are looking for a Monique White. There's a few questions that we need to ask her."One of the officers said.

Monique was nervous as she opened the door. "Come in sir. I am Monique. The officer stepped into the living room and said, "Ma'am. I'm sorry to inform you of this, but Creshon Morris was shot to death this morning"

Monique fell to her knees and tears filled her face. She couldn't understand why she had to lose someone close to her again and why did it have to be her boyfriend. Why and how was all she could think about. She was curious so she asked the cops between crying. "So how did you know to come here?"

"Mrs White, your phone number was the last number in Mr Morris's text message thread and that's why we're here to see if you have any information that could possibly lead us to finding his killer."The officer explained.

Tina was curious as to the voices that she heard in the living room, so she made her way downstairs to see just who it was. The two officers had her worried. Tina thought to herself. "I hope this ain't about J.R."She stopped in the living room and asked, "What's going on Monique, and please don't tell me…"Tina's voice was trembling and became weak.

"Mom!" Monique cried out. "Somebody killed Creshon!"

Tina wiped her eyes. She and Monique embraced each other.

"Why mom? Why can't I ever have someone good stay in life?"Monique cried.

Her cries became louder. The officers kept taking notes. After a few more questions one of the officers handed Monica a card and said. "Ma'am if you come up with any information that you think may be helpful, please feel free to give us a call."

For the remainder of the day. Monique stayed to herself in her bedroom. She wondered if Reggie could have pulled something off like this out of retaliation. But would he throw his life away over a car? She didn't think so and it made her second guess her thoughts. However, it didn't make her completely alienate the thought of Reggie doing it.

Monique's phone rang. "Ring Ring Ring!"

"Hello,"Monique answered sadly.

"What's up with you over there? Why you sounding all down?"Fernando said. He could sense that there was a problem.

"The cops just left. They said that somebody killed Creshon this morning."

Fernando couldn't believe his ears.

Monique continued, "And I'm not really in the mood for a whole lot of talking right now."

There was a silence between the two of them.

"Did they say where it happened?"Fernando asked. "I hope it wasn't by our house,"he continued.

"And for your information J.R., no it wasn't by our house!"Monique said angrily. "And since that's all you're worried about, I'm good with this conversation."

"Whoa sis! I didn't mean it like that. I just want to make sure that you and Ma are all right."

"Bye J.R.,"Monique said and hung up the phone before he could finish speaking.

DARK TINT FILLED his windows to keep unknown individuals out of his business, and those who were familiar with him to wonder who else occupied the vehicle. With the windows rolled up and fog lights on in the daytime, Fernando looked very important to some degree. Especially in Edgewood Court. Deon was looking forward to going back to the storage unit. This time he wouldn't be looking around, he was just going to grab the things he needed to add-on to his hustle. But there was a sudden change of plans thanks to Monique. Deon was sitting on the front stoop smoking and talking to his new neighbor. She had moved into Nicole's old apartment and Deon was trying to get her acquainted with the neighborhood. After word got back to Nichole about her boyfriend. She was gone with the wind, leaving everything behind including her job. A lot of people are happy, but she left someone behind that was still curious about her.

"I'm going to get up with your fine ass later,"Deon said to the new neighbor as he stood up.

"Okay,"she said as she walked off, giving him a perfect view of everything that he was intending on getting.

She had a thin waist, a heart-shaped ass that jiggled with every step she took.

"Damn!"Deon said and shook his head.

Then his attention was drawn to Fernando's porsche. The door flung open.

"What's good fam?"Deon said and then hopped in the passenger seat.

"It's a lot going on right now bro, so that storage thing gone have to wait until tomorrow,"Fernando said. "I'm so sick of so much bullshit. He continued."And you don't know the half of it," he said and then pulled off.

"What the fuck Nicole done did now! I thought shawty got the hell on?"

"Naw, not shawty. But while it's on my mind you remember that letter she left?"Fernando said.

"You talking about the one you been supposed to told me about?"Deon asked.

"On the real bra, I've been going through it. If it ain't one thing it's another with me."Fernando said and paused. He continued saying, "But anyways Nicole crazy ass is now claiming that we are brother and sister. She said her dad was having an affair with my mom,"Fernando said shaking his head and being in denial at the thought.

"That's deeper than rap bro. But like for real though that's something you can't let go. You need to bypass her and hit up Nasty," Deon advised.

"I was thinking about that, but just ain't built up the courage to follow through with it. I was saying that I needed a vacation to convince myself to go out west."Fernando said.

"Damn my nigga!"Deon sighed. "I don't know what else to tell you."

"I do. I got to get the hell out of Dodge for a while," Fernando said and then jumped in his ride and hit the expressway.

REGGIE'S WHEREABOUTS FROM daybreak to noon weighed heavily on Monique's mind. She stared at her phone as if Reggie was about to appear through the receiver.

"Should I call him?"Monique thought to herself, then the thought of his girlfriend picking up the phone made her second guess her decision. Her bedroom door was open. Her attention was drawn down the hall in the direction of her mother's room. She wondered who was sitting at the edge of her bed.

"Maybe she can call for me?"Monique thought to herself and then shouted, "Mom!"

"I'm painting my fingernails girl, what is it?"Monique walked up to her wearing a fake smile.

Tina was so eager to rebuild their bond that she was willing to do anything to get back in her daughter's good graces.

"Can I ask you a question mom?"Monique said.

"Sure!"Tina responded.

"I know this might sound crazy, but I need to talk to you about Reggie. It's a serious matter."Tina propped up and prepared for what seemed to be some bad news.

"You ain't got to look that way, because I'm not pregnant. If that's what you were thinking."Monique explained.

Tina exhales with a smile. "Thank God,"she said.

"Would you mind calling Reggie for me mom? I am asking because you know if I hear a little Misses Whitey's voice! I'm bound to snap,"Monique said.

"Pass me my phone,"Tina said.

Monique leaned across the bed and watched her mom get ready to dial the number.

"What's the number?"Tina asked.

She kissed her daughter on the forehead as she dialed the number. Tina nodded her head as she said, "Hello Reggie?"

"Yes,"Reggie answered with a raspy voice.

"How have you been darling? This is Monique's mother, Mrs. White."

He sounds surprised as he said, "I didn't recognize your voice at first because you and Monique sound so similar over the phone. But I am fine Mrs. White and how about yourself?"Reggie continued.

"The good Lord blesses us everyday young man!"Tina responded.

Monique was becoming anxious and she began sighing and breathing heavily waiting for her mom to get to her point. And without another word Tina handed Monique the phone and silently mouthed, "Here you go."

Monique looked at the phone for a minute before she actually spoke.

"Reggie,"she stuttered. "This is Monique and before you hang up, can you hear me out real quick?"

"I'm listening,"Reggie said.

"Well, if your company doesn't have you occupied right now, can you meet me at the *Starbucks* across from *Lenox Mall* in 30 minutes?"

"What company are you referring to Monique? I'm here alone."

The phone went silent.

"What time do you want to meet?"Reggie said.

FERNANDO SAW HIS sister as she was trying to exit the driveway, heading to meet Reggie. He flashed his headlights at her so that she could back up. He approached her hoping that Creshon wasn't the one who had to bite the bullet. Before Fernando could start talking, Monique went on and on saying that she was in a hurry. Fernando knew that they needed to talk. He forcefully insisted and promised not to take more than 10 minutes of her time. Deon stepped out of the car once he saw Monique complying.

"Good to see you again, Monique,"Deon said.

She waved camly and walked back into the house.

"Where is Ma at?"Fernando asked, hoping to break the ice.

"Probably in her skin J.R.! Now come on what's so important? And don't forget I got some place to be!"Monique pleaded.

Deon walked past them and headed into the living room. Monique and Fernando's conversation escalated and began to get loud as they talked.

"Why are you running back to that clown? Do you know how stupid that makes you look?"Fernando asked.

"I hope it's not as bad as you and Mom not telling me about Reggie cheating on me,"Monique waited for an answer. "I know that's right! You didn't think I'd find out huh?"She continued to shout. "You of all people J.R., I figured at least you would have put your little sister up on game. But that's cool. God got my back. And whoever killed Creshon at that store is going to have to answer to somebody one day."She pointed in his face. "Mark my words."She left him standing with his head low and his mouth open.

Deon walked up. "Are you good?"

"Damn bro!"Fernando said loudly.

"That dude this morning. This shit is all bad, Deon!" Fernando nodded.

"Look at it like this Nando. Oh boy had to be on some slime shit to be following you in the first place."Deon said.

"I know. But now this, and then Alex,"Fernando said.

Tina cleared her throat as she came down the steps. "Now what's this about Alex?"

"Um Um,"Fernando cleared his throat and looked at Deon as if he could help.

"I was saying that it's sad what happened to him and now this."He said, trying to keep his lie as straight as possible. Because he knew his mother would eventually catch on.

"Excuse us for a minute, Deon,"Tina said curiously.

Deon went to the car. He figured that there was definitely about to be some smoke between the two of them. Sit down J.R. She kept her eye on him.

"Before you say anything son, I want you to know that I was at the top of the steps listening to the whole conversation. So if there's something you need to tell me please be straight up because I'm your Mom first and there's nothing you can say that will keep me from being on your side,"She said as she rubbed his back to relax him.

He kept his head down. Finally he looked up and gave his mom a long hug. Detail by detail he told her how Alex robbed him and he also told her about the situation with Creshon. After talking to his mom about the situations he felt better. He knew he had some errands to run and he knew that he needed to bounce, so he left. Tina stood in the doorway as Fernando backed out of the driveway, praying that he would have a safe journey. She went back inside of the house and closed the door behind her. She stopped at the bar and grabbed a bottle of rum. Tina then went to her room and ended up being locked in there and drowning herself in pain.

REGGIE PULLED UP to *Lenox Mall* and parked his brand new Mercedes-Benz AMG. He was dressed to the tee in his tailored *Tom Ford* suit. He smelled good in his *Givenchy* cologne. He knew that the impression that he was making had to be a memorable one for his ex. Monique was looking her best. She was dressed to impress in some of the finest threads that money could buy, because she wasn't your average girl.

Reggie's tinted windows made it hard for her to recognize who was driving the two-door Benz. Reggie blew his horn. Honk Honk! He let his passenger window down just enough so that Monique could see his face. He smiled. Monique loved his smile and seeing him made it hard for her to stay focused and she knew it.

"Nice car," she said as she sat inside.

She glanced around at all of the gadgets in the vehicle and said, "Listen Reggie, I'm going to get straight to the point. What did I do wrong to deserve being cheated on? I fed and fucked you whenever you wanted it, then on top of that, I put up with all of your long ass working hours. Be honest and please tell me what I did wrong to deserve this?"Monique sat there anxious to hear his response.

Reggie exhaled deeply because he knew that the question would surface eventually but he didn't think it would be this soon.

"Honestly, you're as perfect as they come, Mo," he began. "It was all me and my doggish nature. I knew that, and that's not an excuse. That's why I'll take all the blame. Listen Monique, I'm glad we're finally talking because I've been wanting to tell you how very sorry I am for hurting you sweetheart. Women like you deserve much more."Reggie reached over and grabbed her hand, looked her in the eyes and continued. "Will you ever find it in your heart to forgive me?"

Her heart warmed up to his words. She shook her head from left to right. But in her mind before they took another step, Reggie had to prove his whereabouts during the time of Creshon's death.

"I'm not content with holding grudges Reggie. I just don't want my feelings to blind me and then I end up hurt again."she said and pulled her hand away."Are you and your friend still... you know?"

"Naw, she's been gone ever since that fucked up incident and situation the other night." Reggie said.

"So were you in a car accident or something Reggie?" Monique said, sounding naive and concerned.

"Naw girl, not a car accident Monique, someone broke into my house and robbed us.""They tied us up, cleaned out my safe and then took my car. After all of that was over, she left me and didn't look back."Reggie said.

In his frustration, he started hitting the steering wheel.

"But there was one good thing that did come out of the situation,"Reggie said.

Monique was curious about what Reggie meant by that. She did her best concealing her emotions, and she was upset that Creshon went against her wishes and didn't listen to her and that made her blood pressure rise back up.

In Monique's mind, Reggie definitely was the one who killed Creshon she thought. She began asking questions.

"How long have you had this car?"She asked, seeming concerned even though she wasn't.

"I just got it this morning. Why you ask?"

"I wasn't asking for any particular reason, I was just curious."she said.

Monique hesitated and then asked. "While we're here, can you grab me my favorite drink?"

Reggie looked up and checked out the coffee line. It was short so he asked, "Green mint or peppermint? I know how you are about your coffee."

"Green Mint, and thank you."

Reggie got out of the vehicle and went to get Monique some coffee. Monique needed answers and fast about what happened to Creshon. She thought to herself, "Where were you?"

When Reggie got out of the car, Monique began searching his vehicle.

"If he was actually at the dealership this morning, then paperwork should still be in here but where?"She said to herself.

Monique searched in the console, the back seat, and in his briefcase, which only had two folders for two of his patients inside of it.

Monique looked up and saw that Reggie was at the cash register and she realized that she had one last shot to try to find something she could use. Monique checked the dashboard compartment, inside was the paperwork with the ticket price of the car on it. Monique scrolled down the paper looking over all of the dates, times and numbers. She checked her Michael Kors watch to make sure that both the date and time were accurate. Monique glanced up and noticed that Reggie was standing outside of the vehicle waiting for her to unlock the door.

"You must have been day dreaming or something? Are you good? I called your name twice,"he said.

"Yeah I'm good. I'm just sitting here thinking about us,"Monique responded.

Reggie looked at her and knew that money was one of her weaknesses but everything about Monique was like kryptonite to him.

"Oh yeah!"His tone made her laugh on the inside.

"I was thinking,"he ran his hand over his neatly shaved goat-tee.

"Would it be somehow possible to take you out sometime soon?"He paused waiting for her response..

Let me think about it. She leaned over and started at the side of his mouth with her tongue then found the entrance. They kissed. Monique felt a relief on the inside, She knew Reggie wasn't a killer. She initially thought that it was him who killed Creshon. However, Reggie being a killer didn't fit his style because Monique knew that Reggie wouldn't kill nothing or let nothing die.

# CHAPTER 13

## Photo Shoot

IT WAS A NORMAL Sunday…The weather was fair and uncertain and Fernando was setting up to do what he loved to do, and that was take pictures and use his keen eye to always put his mind at ease when he started to drift off into daydreams. Fernando was happy to have finally found the time to pick back up his camera.

Fernando clicked on his laptop and he noticed that he had a total of 12 unread messages waiting on him. A few of them were from known photo editors that dated back a week ago and were tagged *Urgent Females Needed.* He decided to skip the interviewing and just schedule a few quick sessions with the regulars.

The morning sky was powder blue and just right for Fernando and his three female models. He needed a good location to shoot his models. The first shoot he had scheduled was for a group called *Str8 Stunna's.* They were an urban organization. Fernando chose the right spot to photograph the models. He chose Maddox Park and it was open to the public. On most weekends, the park was packed, but on that day, the usual crowd had not filled the park yet.

The female models wore the *Urban Outfitter* clothing brand and Fernando made sure all three of them were laced in a pair of *Christian Louboutins* red bottom heels to show that the hood may be Urban but still had class and cash.

One of the models whose name was *Amber* strutted her way towards Fernando with her sexy walk. She said to him,

"Fernando, I aint trying to be funny, but you need to forget waiting on more people to show up because those clouds look like it might be raining soon."

"I know right because I just got my hair done," another one of the models added.

"Well If y'all want to half step and not get the best shots, then that's on yall, let's do it," Fernando said, not happy. Because he hated doing things halfway, and that was one of his pet peeves.

Amber applied more makeup to her face because of the lighting outside and afterwards she helped the other models with their makeup as well.

As Fernando adjusted the lights preparing them for the shoot, he felt somebody staring at him.

It was Amber standing there with her arms folded in disgust. She snapped at Fernando saying, "Are you done yet? Because all of these trashy beer cans out here stank. Why don't they clean this park up more often?"

Fernando ignored her comment and then said out loud, "Perfect! Let's do it!"He began looking through the lens on the camera to check the focus.

Fernando began taking pictures of the models. He started with Amber and then after he finished with everyone, he gathered them together for group pictures. Before they knew it, when they looked up, the park was packed with the westside's finest. Because of that, Ferando's photoshoot grew a crowd. The models were getting so much attention that it overwhelmed them.

Struggle decided to pull up to the park that day. He drove a candy painted green Chevelle sitting on a pair of 28 inch *Dubs* through the park and stopped behind the crowded gazebo.

Amber noticed the fly ride and because she was feeling herself she decided to walk towards Struggle's vehicle with a seductive walk as if she was on the catwalk. As she made her way to the vehicle, the camera kept snapping shots.

"Say their Ma!"Struggle yelled out of the window. Unless you trying to hop in, you might want to back up from this wet paint.

"Shhhhh! We're almost done,"Amber whispered as she put her hand up to her lips telling Struggle to be quiet.

Struggle hopped out of his whip and slammed the door. He snatched Amber off of his hood and said, "Bitch you must be deaf, huh?"

Amber was surprised at Struggle's reaction. She shook her head from left to right rapidly.

"Well since you acted like you couldn't hear me the first time, I guessed that you were trying to hop in."

He tried to force her into the passenger seat, however, it wasn't easy.

Amber kicked and screamed. "Please, stop please!"

"Naw bitch, don't resist now,"Struggle yelled.

Fernando ran up and smashed his camera on the back of Struggles head! "Awwwwww!"Struggle yelled as the camera went across his head.

WHEN FERNANDO CAME to, he was in a hospital bed. Three people were sitting on a bench across from his bed. Fernando thought that he was dreaming. He sat there for a moment in a daze trying to remember everything that took place. A couple hours had passed since he had been out cold, but to him it seemed like a whole year. He started shaking his head from side to side in confusion.

"Mrs. White,"Deon said as he nugged her. "He's moving, should I get the nurse?"

"Yes! Hurry!"Tina said as she jumped up.

Deon left the hospital room to go and get a nurse.

"What hap……"Fernando tried to say as he swallowed and then opened his mouth trying to speak.

Tina started crying.

Deon came back into the room with the nurse and she began checking Fernando's vital signs.

"Where is Amber?"Fernando says as he tried to sit up.

"Amber, was shot two times in the chest Fernando."Deon said and then paused. "She died on her way here to the hospital."

"Fuck! Fuck!"Fernando screamed.

He looked around in distress and said, "What about the other women?"

Monique jumped in and said, "They say you and Amber were the only two that suffered from gunshot wounds. J. R. I want to know that I'm so glad that you are still here with us."Monique said as she broke down crying and wraps her arms around his neck.

For the next two weeks, Fernando was laid up in the hospital room all alone, not wanting to be bothered, but his wishes didn't stop the countless amount of flowers and surprise pop up visits that he got.

One surprise he did get was from two detectives. They reminded him of the two cops from the show 'CHiPs' . Fernando almost laughed out loud when he saw them but he kept it to himself. The officer kept asking question after question about the shooter even though he had been killed. Fernando guessed that they felt like black on black crime wasn't complete unless both parties were dead or either in jail.

Fernando pleaded the fifth and said nothing. He laid in the bed thinking to himself,

"Better luck next time fellas."

# CHAPTER 14

## The Molly Made Me Do It

DIAMONDS OF ATLANTA was having a memorial party for Amber. There were a lot of signs that read *Rest in Peace Amber.* There were strippers from all over Atlanta in attendance.

Fernando was injured and couldn't be at his best, but Deon knew how to kick flavor for the both of them due to the sauce that his buddy Nando had been dripping on him for so long.

"Pipe it up! Pipe it up!"The music blasted out of the sound system as Deon swaggered through the crowd wearing *Ralph Lauren's Purple Label* from head to toe. He was fresh to death and he was feeling himself however, there was one thing missing and that was his ace, boon, coon Fernando.

"Hey Deon!" Denise said as she walked up checking him out from head to toe. "I thought y'all was gonna be a no show. Where is Fernando?"she asked.

"He ain't feeling well, I think he ate something that didn't agree with him." Deon lied.

"Oh okay I'm sorry to hear that. Well tell him that I asked about him and I hope he gets better soon."Denise said, empathically.

"Okay I will."Deon said and walk off shaking his head.

It seemed as if everyone in the club was missing Fernando. Just about everyone asked where he was. Deon gave each one of them a different story of his whereabouts. He made his way to the VIP area and stiff armed everyone that asked him about Fernando.

The D J got on the mic and said, "We're going to switch it up a bit tonight. We have a special guest in the house and this young man came through to pay his respects to the one and only Lady Ice! Rest in peace Lady Ice. He truly needs no introduction, I want everyone to give it up for Lil Mexico's own.. Meathead!"

The crowd went crazy and cheered as Meathead grabbed the mic.

Meathead announced, "I like to dedicate this song to my big bro and OG. Also to the beautiful, and well respected queen. Ms. Lady Ice!"

The lights dimmed, and then Meathead's alter ego kicked in. He came alive as he rapped his song. "Hardly, Hardly, Hardly-we miss you, yeeeeaaah!" Meathead went into beast mode.

Deon peeped out of the VIP area at Meathead as he performed and they both made eye contact with each other. Deon sighed and saluted Meathead as he paid his respect.

Deon wasn't sure if it was the weed that was making him feel what he was feeling or what. But when he saw this beautiful lady walking in, he noticed that when she stopped, so did the eyes of everyone else because she was flawless. Her mini skirt hugged her hips and all of the right places all the way down to her juicy thighs. Once Deon recognized who she was, he began remembering their encounter at the hotel, however he just couldn't remember her looking that glamourous.

Once Jennifer got closer to Deon, she spoke to him in a sexy tone of voice saying, "Hey Papi! I am surprised to be seeing you again so soon!"

"Well I'm glad to be seeing you so soon! Are you alone or did you come with someone?" Deon asked as he was checking her out.

"I left the girls at home this time. Do you need some company Papi? Si?"Jennifer asked.

"Now how can I ever turn down some company with you. Deon said as he bit his bottom lip."Have a seat and fix us a drink. I got to make a blunt run to the restroom aight mami?"

Jennifer nodded with a sexy smile and did as he said.

WHEN DEON RETURNED, Jennifer was hugged up with a beautiful chocolate stallion. Her hair was long and wavy and when she sat down it looked as if she was sitting on two basketballs.

Jennifer noticed that Deon was watching them so she turned the volume up.

She said to him, "Look what I've found. I got us some chocolate dessert. And I love everything dark."

Both women began kissing passionately. Deon looked at the women kissing and his nature immediately rose. He drunk the drink in his hand and then immediately poured himself another.

HE THOUGHT TO himself, "This is about to be a long night."

Deon sat between both women and wondered to himself which one of the fine ass women was going to get it first.

HOLLYWOOD PULLED UP to the spot and he was geeked out of his mind. He had snorted a few lines and it had him feeling like he was the Incredible Hulk. He paid the bouncer an extra fifty dollars to let him slide through the door with his pistol. Because he was wearing a loose fitted Gucci hoodie it made it easier for him to conceal his weapon from the crowd. The dancers were asking him if he wanted a dance, but Hollywood kept saying no because he wasn't distracted by all of the pussy surrounding, because he was on a mission and it wasn't to celebrate Lady Ice like everyone else was.

The night before, Hollywood got stiffed for a few thousand and his sources pointed him to what was supposed to be one of the biggest parties of the year. So he figured that his target would be there partying it up like everyone else.

Hollywood stood at the bar and ordered a bottle and a line of Molly, and  while standing at the bar he noticed one of the waitresses when he looked up.

"Aye Kesha what up girl!" Hollywood said.

Kesha stopped in mid stride and responded, "Hollywood, oh I didn't even recognize that was you with that hoodie on."

Kesha was lying. She asked him, "Who the hell are you trying to hide from?"

"Bitch, when have you ever heard of Hollywood running or hiding from anybody, huh?"He said as he grabbed Kesha by her neck.

"Aaaaahhhh…let me go! You're hurting me Hollywood!"Kesha cried out.

"I should slap your dumb ass for standing me up last week! But I ain't gone do that because I love the way you say my name. So when you gonna make it up to me sexy?"Hollywood said.

Before she had a chance to answer, he pushed her out of the way at the sight of his target. "Bingo!"he said to himself.

When Hollywood became distracted, Kesha took the opportunity to escape into the crowd. Hollywood stayed at the bar and kept his eyes on his target. He noticed that his target was on the move, so Hollywood just laid in the cut and watched his targets every move until he thought it was the right time to pounce on his prey.

JENNIFER LOOKED OVER her shoulder and winked at Deon and continued heading to the restroom.

"Have you made arrangements for after the club yet?"The stripper asked Deon.

"From the way your friend is talking, she has already kidnapped me for the night,"he continued.

Well, when Jen gets back, we gone leave this spot and fall up in the telly, what you think?" Deon said.

"Think about what papi?"Jennifer asked as she returned.

"Jen, you're just in time baby. We were just talking about you and how tonight's going to end." Deon said.

"I hope you said something sexy," She cooed while rubbing his crotch.

Jennifer plopped down next to the dancer, and threw one leg up on her lap.

"We were waiting on you girl, shit we are ready to dip." The stripper said eagerly.

Deon looked at the stripper and said, "Get dressed and meet us at the bar!"

HOLLYWOOD PULLED DOWN his hoodie and snorted another line off of his hand before coming out of the shadows. It was time to ride. In the parking lot, he thought the Molly had him tripping when he stood looking from a distance at three bodies getting into the Range Rover that he knew was Fernando's truck, without Fernando in sight.

"These fools tripping! Where the fuck is my nigga at? He said to himself while wiping his nose."These mother fuckers must want some smoke."

And Hollywood was with all the smoke. He was in a zone and he became enraged at the thought of someone having Fernando's truck.

Deon was happy as hell to be headed to the hotel with the two sexy sisters. He was so focused on what he wanted to do with the women sexually that he wasn't paying any attention to his surroundings and realizing that he was being followed. Deon merged onto the highway, and Hollywood followed behind him a few cars back. The traffic began to die down and Hollywood looked around and scanned the expressway to make sure that the coast was clear so that he could execute his plan.

Hollywood looked around and saw that there were no other cars in sight at the moment, so he hit the gas and pulled up on the side of the Range Rover. He opened fire into the vehicle, shattering the passenger side front and back windows. Deon swerved the truck off of the road crashing it into an embankment. The truck came to a halt and Hollywood pulled over by the vehicle so that he could see who had the nerve to take his partnas Range Rover. He also had a habit of wanting to make sure that the job was done so he had to go and see for himself.

Hollywood walked up to the wreckage and snatched the driver side door open. Deon fell out of the vehicle hyperventilating and clutching his neck. Deon was gasping for air and he no longer felt the high of being untouchable that he had been feeling earlier that evening. It was all crashing down at that moment and he couldn't stop it, because his number in life had been called and it was time to meet his maker. He looked up at Hollywood and said in his last breaths, "Not the homie!"

Deon collapses after uttering his final words in disbelief. The two women were still alive. They were panicking and moaning as they squirmed in pain. Hollywood notices and sends two shots to their heads putting their lights out and leaving no witnesses. Hollywood shook his head as he stared at Deon's lifeless body. He was geeked out of his mind and so many thoughts ran through his head.

He thought to himself, "What in the fuck am I going to tell Fernando?"

# CHAPTER 15

## The Arena

One month later…

FERNANDO'S RECOVERY DIDN'T come as quick as others had expected it to. He was still in shock with PTSD over Deon's death, not to mention the trauma of him also being shot. To top that off, his sister Monique had revealed to him that she was pregnant and a mother to be. She hit him with some news that was gut wrenching when she told him that the father of her child was Creshon. Once he heard that devastating news he was blown away and the drama behind all of this definitely felt like a moment from the Jerry Springer Show.

Fernando sat alone and thought about a dream that he once had. The thought of the dream made him say to himself, "I'm definitely leaving now."

His phone vibrates, bizz, bizz, bizz!

He eased out of his bed, still sore as he reached for his phone. He had a text message.

The message read: "My nigga, I hope you're feeling better. Man…my bad for not pulling up on you at the hospital and shit. I've been on the go like a mother fucka. Bro, I came up on two Atlanta Hawks tickets and if you want to roll with me that . Bro! You gotta get out of that bed! Lol! Hit me up and let me know what's up."

Hollywood.

Fernando tossed the phone back on the nightstand after reading a text. He thought about Hollywood's offer but because he had been out of the races for a while, it had him in a "I don't give a fuck mood."His facial hair had grown all the way out, his waves had not been brushed. His shower schedule was way off and he didn't smell the best. He got up and looked in the mirror.

He said to himself, "Pull yourself together my nigga!"

After showering, Fernando ate a snack and then he headed to *Langford's Barber Shop* in *Kirkwood.* When he got there, it was too crowded so he went to the next barbershop on the east side called *Ironhead Cuts.* Ironhead was always packed but when Fernando showed up, the crowd either had to wait on him, or reschedule their appointments. And that's just how it was.

Darrell was Fernando's barber and when he saw Fernando's red and black mustang pulling up into the parking lot, he rushed to finish up the kid that sat in a chair and gave him the fastest low fade that his mom had ever seen.

Once Fernando walked into the shop, he greeted everybody and then took a seat into Darrell's chair. Fernando knew that he was looking rough but he was relieved that he finally was putting himself back together.

Once Fernando sat down, Darrell shouted, "Listen up! Listen up! I am sorry to say this but I'm going to have to close down for a while, but we reopen around……"he checked his watch and continued, "Check back around three o clock, sorry for the inconvenience everyone."

The customers inside mumbled to themselves disappointed as they exited the barbershop.

"Fam, I could've waited until you finished with everyone. I know I look rough bro, but I ain't in no hurry."Fernando said.

"It's all good Fernando, you want to know the truth, I need a break. I need to smoke me one like yesterday because I've been at it since like 8:00 this morning. Shit I need it in my life."Darrell said laughing.

"Well, If you got a blunt. I got the weed,"Fernando said and then paused as a notification popped up on his phone.

He opened the message and it read: Friend request accepted by H.N.I.C RED better known as *Nasty Red.*

Fernando left a message in Nasty Red's inbox. It read: Meet and greet. I need your number ASAP.

Darrell noticed that Fernando was bothered by something that he had just read so he asked him, "You good big homie?"

"Yeah, I'm aight, but would you believe me if I told you that I might have another sister that I didn't know about? And to top it off, White might not be my father."

Darrell was caught off guard by the news.

He said, "Damn bra! So what do you plan on doing? And how do you plan on confronting the sources that you got the information from?"

"I hadn't fully thought everything through yet. However, I did make plans to hit the West Coast so that I see what's up over there. All I am waiting on is the directions for when I get there,"Fernando inhaled and continued, "And as for my ma dukes, I ain't going to say nothing to her until everything is confirmed.""Until then, I am just going to focus on my first priority."

"Okay that's what's up O.G. Well good luck fam. And I pray that everything works out in your favor,"Darrell said.

Fernando nodded as he acknowledged Darrell's empathetic comment.

Hollywood and Fernando met each other at the same time at the State Farm Arena. The parking lot was jam-packed; they paid for parking and then headed inside to their courtside floor seats. The Hawks Arena was lit and the fans had that fever. The energy was amazing, as fans screamed and shouted as Harry the Hawk entertained them. Fans wore their signature jerseys and hats to match. The Hawks were playing the Lakers, and LeBron always brought out a huge crowd.

"How in hell did you manage to grab some floor seats? Fernando asked Hollywood as they moved through the crowd.

"Let's just say I know somebody that knows somebody," Hollywood grinned.

"Say no mo then fam!" Fernando replied

~~~

IT WAS HALFTIME and the Hawks had a 10 point lead. Fernando started rubbing his hands together with a mischievous grin on his face at the thought of a victory by The Hawks. When the home team went down by 20 points early on in the game, Hollywood decided to bet Fernando a stack thinking that it was a sucka bet however Fernando accepted it.

"Why in the fuck did I go against the home team!" Hollywood thought to himself as he sat there watching the Hawks come back and take the lead.

"Bro these beers got me full, and I gotta piss. I'll be right back,"Fernando said.

He paused then and then asked Hollywood, "Which side did we pass the restrooms on?"Hollywood pointed to the left. Fernando got up and began walking alongside the court during the halftime show. He passed a lot of familiar faces, there was *T.I.*, *Bobby Valentino*, *Ludacris*, and *Buffy the Body.* Fernando almost tripped over her red bottom heels. Even though he felt a bit of embarrassment, Fernando still managed to get a second look at her body.

The lobby was crowded during halftime and luckily Fernando could see bathroom signs. Fernando finally got a chance to relieve himself. He washed his hands and headed back to his seat but before he reached the stairs, two women cut him off. The weed and the few beers he drank had him slightly staggering. Fernando stepped back and composed himself so he could put a name with their faces.

"Pappi, I hope we didn't leave a bad impression the last time we were together, No?" Martina asked. Carmine whispered in his ear, "Ooooh I remember that!"as she pointed at his dick and then giggled.

"Yeah! Now I remember y'all."He said as he checked them out. "The Doubletree."But last time it was three of y'all.. where is.. Jennifer?"

Both women looked confused and hunch their shoulders as if they were saying that they didn't know what happened to her.
~~~

Then Carmine nodded at Martina giving her the go ahead to speak.

She said, "How about we have our own halftime show?"

"Where? In here?" Fernando asked.

"No silly, in our truck outside! And if we go now we won't take too long, trust me,"Martina said seductively.

Her tone of voice and looks had Fernando getting weak at the knees.

HOLLYWOOD CHECKED HIS watch and then looked up at the scoreboard. It was 5 minutes into the third quarter and he began to wonder about Fernando's whereabouts."Where is this fool at?"he said to himself. He began looking around to see if he saw Fernando. Finally he noticed Fernando heading towards the exit with two women by his side. Hollywood was surprised to see his friend trying to have some fun without him so he rushed towards Fernando and the young ladies following them to their destination.

Hollywood finally made it to the parking lot where he noticed the two young ladies trying to get Fernando to get in the truck so that they could serve him up. He could tell that Fernando wanted to cuff the girls and keep them all to himself, but Hollywood wasn't going for that. And to top it off, he noticed that one of the girls was Latino, and Hollywood loved himself some mamasitas for sure, even though his love for hispanic women had got him in plenty of trouble.

Hollywood pulled up and surprised them saying, "Well, well, well! What do we have here?"

Carmine turned her nose up at the site of Hollywood and Martina jumped in the truck without saying a word.

Fernando looked at Hollywood and smirked. He says, " I know, I know, I know, but bro, it was a spur of the moment thing and…."

Mamacita, I hope you don't mind if Big Daddy joins in for the fun! "Hollywood said, interrupting Fernando and grabbing one of Carmine's breasts.

"Stop! "Carmine said as she stepped back, pushing Hollywood's hand away.

"Fernando, we are out of here because this dude is a creep," she said and jumped in the passenger seat. She rolled down the window and said, "When you have time, use the number that I gave you and make sure you're alone next time."

FERNANDO TURNED AROUND and broke out laughing. "Ha Ha Fool, you be pulling up side ways on them hoes. You know only a sista would understand your swag. But these foreign chicks only understand dollar signs."

"You think?" Hollywood asked.

Fernando thought that he was seeing things and tripping when he noticed the truck pulling back up.

He said to Hollywood,"It seemed like my girls must have changed their minds."

Hollywood had always been on his P's and Q's so he had peeped the move. He grabbed Fernando and forced him to the ground to shield him from the gun fire that began to erupt. Bullets shattered the windshield. Hollywood crawled on the ground and stayed low and made his way back to his car. He opened his car door and reached for his Glock 40. Once he got it into hand he returned fire sending the shooters a message letting them know that he ain't nothing to be played with.

The truck stopped and the reverse lights came on and started heading his way. The sound that came from the weapons that the enemy were shooting sounded like bombs coming from their weapons. Hollywood didn't stand a chance with his semi automatic weapon.

He said a prayer, "God please help me!"Then he came out blasting.

Hollywood heard additional shots being fired close by. He recognized that it was Fernando coming from the opposite side wiping out both shooters. Hollywood felt a sense of reprieve after Fernando came to the rescue. Once the shooting stopped, they jumped in Hollywood's *Challenger* and hauled ass.

The Next Day……

TINA WAS CHILLING with a glass of wine as she watched T.V. She noticed the words *Breaking News* as it popped up on the screen. Tina turned up the volume so that she could hear what the breaking news was. Monique was in the kitchen preparing a meal.

She shouted from the kitchen and said, "Have you heard anything from J.R yet? Because I've been calling that boy since yesterday."

She shook her head and continued, "That boy gets on my last nerves,"she thought to herself as she walked to the living room.

She was in shock as she looked at the T.V. She said surprised, "Ma! Look who's face is on the news!"

THE NEWS ANCHOR said, "Late Breaking News….There are two suspects on the run after two victims were found dead on the scene. We don't have the names of the victims at this time, but as soon as we get all of the details we will update you with them. Detectives are viewing the surveillance footage of the crime scene."

A SHADOW MOVED through the wooded yard swiftly in order to accomplish its mission. Twigs snapped and leaves crunched as the person's stride became more and more intense. This was an important mission and a lot was at stake. There were a lot of questions about why things had to be the way they were and one way or another someone and something had to be accountable for providing answers. "What the f***!"The person quickly ducked behind a wheelbarrow to get out of view. With the help of a 5-ft wide oak tree, it made it impossible to see the shadow lurking in the dark. it was the cops patrolling the area and cruising down the driveway, they were not looking around and being suspicious however they were in the area.

~~~

THE OFFICERS DRILLED Tina with question after question to try and get her to tell them about Fernando's whereabouts. The officer had probable cause and searched the house without a warrant. The officers left after coming up empty handed. Fernando was nowhere in sight. After a twenty minute search of the premise, the officers ended their search and gave Tina notice about them returning again soon.

Once the officers left, everything fell on the house like a ton of bricks. Tina fainted at the fact that her son was a wanted man. She was out cold and It felt like she was in an episode of The First 48.

Boom! Boom! Boom! Boom! Boom! Boom! was the sound that Monique heard at the door as she tried to help her mother regain consciousness. Monique's first mind told her that it was probably more cops trying to harass them so more. As Tina began to come around, Monique rushed to the front door and snatched it open with an attitude. She was angry about how they had treated her and her mother while trashing their home. What do you want? She yelled as she opened the door. Her facial expression turned sour at the site of the female standing on the other side of the door. The two women stared each other down with disdain in their eyes. Before either one could utter a word, a gun shot rang out from within the house forcing the visitor to take off running away from the house.
~~~

# CHAPTER 16

## To Live and Die in L. A

FERNANDO WOKE UP when he heard the flight attendant announcing that they were about to land. When he opened his eyes, he noticed how the mountains kissed the skyline. Chills ran down his spine. "Welcome to the sunny state of California. Have a safe and wonderful trip everyone. Thank you for flying Delta," the flight attendant said.

Fernando got through the traffic and grabbed his bags at baggage claim and held him in an executive Town car to take him to his location. The 98° weather felt beautiful on his skin as he jumped into the vehicle ready to tour the city of dreams. Fernando payed attention to how each area changed depending on what part of town they were in. The driver explained to him that the city was working hard to gain it's tourist attraction status back. The driver was a great tour guide for Fernando, and even though the ride was about an hour long, it didn't seem like it due to the great information about the city that the tour guide provided.

The driver took a turn onto a graveled road that went up a hill. Fernando noticed that the driver had to go slow so that the vehicle could keep its traction. Fernando looked out of the window and noticed that they were high in the hills and things began to look smaller down below as they kept going up. He said to himself, "Damn, how high is this place? Shit, everything looks so damn small right now."

The driver said, "Well, everything is small from up here. This is Sherman Oaks." They finally reached the destination and Fernando admired how elegant and extravagant the estate was. He noticed how the home was centered in the middle of large palm trees and a rose garden. Fernando remained quiet as the driver approached the gated estate. The driver stopped the car and put it in park. He got out of the vehicle and opened the door for Fernando. He patted him on his back and smiled.

Fernando looked up at the palatial estate and thought to himself, "Wow! This is really nice!"He was a bit nervous and the closer to the door his stomach started to feel like knots were in it. He made it to the front door and before he could ring the doorbell it opened.

Nasty Red yelled with excitement, "Fernando! Welcome! Welcome! Come on in! I am glad you made it! Follow me this way!"

As they walked, Fernando said in awe as he looked up at the antique chandeliers, "This shit is like a hood dream."

They made it to a pair of double doors that lead to the formal dining area. The table was being prepared by a private chef and he was placing a platter of skewered jerk chicken, coconut shrimp, caviar that had been imported, and spicy crab cakes. Everything looked perfect Fernando thought to himself.

As they were about to sit down to eat, a beautiful woman entered the dining room. Fernando looks up as she speaks to Nasty.

She says with aggravation and concern in her tone, "I've been calling your name and looking for you for the last past hour. Did you just get here?"

Monea was Nasty's girlfriend. She had been his girlfriend and acquaintance for a little over a year. To him, she was sexy and he liked her because she didn't demand too much. He met Monea in Jamaica. Nasty was stunned by her beauty so much that he thought to himself that he just had to bring her back to the States, and so he did. Monea was gorgeous and accepting of all of Nasty's ways. She knew that he was a drug dealer and because of that fact, she knew that being with a drug dealer wasn't easy for anyone. However, being with a drug dealer in the States was better than the lifestyle that she had in Jamaica, so when Nasty asked her to come back to the states with him, she didn't hesitate to agree or pass up on the opportunity for a better life.

Nasty responded to Monea saying, "I've been here all afternoon, did you forget that I told you earlier that I was having a friend fly in today and that I would be busy with my guest all day?"

She looked at him with a confused look as if she had forgotten and says, well I must have forgotten, but I just got done working out so I'm going to go freshen up."

"Girl I might have to put you on a weed diet or something with the way you are forgetting things,"Nasty said sarcastically.

"I guess so."She said and sashayed off to the bedroom. She waved at Fernando as she turned away.

Nasty looked across the table at Fernando and said to him, let's take a walk.

They began walking through the home and Nasty asked Fernando how things were things were going back in the city?

"What things?"Fernando snapped.

"I mean just things in general. Life. You do have a life don't you?"Nasty responded.

"Bro, I just be cooling. I'm just doing what I can to make some shit shake and stay sucka free,"Fernando said calmly.

As he spoke to Nasty, he was trying to be as calm and vague as possible at the same time.

They made their way to the outdoor patio. They stood there for a moment with a silence between them.

Nasty broke the silence saying,"So bro what's on your mind?"

Fernando was a bit emotional and he felt like a lump was forming in his throat that wouldn't allow him to speak. However he managed to swallow his fear of what he was feeling and speak.

He said to Nasty, "Man! The truth is on my mind. I want the truth! I want to know the truth about everything that has had me blinded for so long."

After sharing how he felt he stood there staring deeply at Nasty, and his stare spoke volumes that needed not be explained and Nasty knew it.

"That ain't gone be no problem,"Nasty said as he stood there reminiscing about that day that changed things. It was all so clear to him, just as if it happened the day before.

IT WAS NEW YEARS DAY and Nasty wanted badly to get a fresh start with Tina. He invited her to Centennial Park so that they could talk. They sat down on a bench by the waterfall and as they sat there, neither one of them knew what to say. Tina just sat there on the bench like a little girl swinging her feet. As the wind blew, it raised her short skirt past her caramel thighs revealing some of her lace front panties. It made her shy so she crossed her legs in embarrassment.

Nasty broke the silence and said, "I've already seen it too many times before so what are you ashamed of?"

"I know but…"Tina said.

"But what? What's up? Nasty became concerned about her sudden insecure demeanor.

I'm getting an abortion she said. I'm five weeks pregnant, and the doctor said that it is not too late for me to make a decision, so don't worry."

Nasty let out a nervous cough. He was choked up and couldn't say the word pregnant.

He asked Tina, "Do you think you could be pregnant by White? Have you told him?"

"No, I haven't told him because I know it's yours. I keep track of my cycle and I am not proud of this. This is all happening so I would just rather let the doctor kill it and get it over with because it's too much for me to handle."

"So it's my baby?"Nasty asked lovingly.

She shook her head acknowledging what he had just asked her.

Nasty stared at her to see if he could pick up on any descent from Tina or if there were any changes in her body language. There wasn't and he didn't sense any cunning ways.

He said to her, "Tina I got money to help you raise the child, and I don't want a dead baby on my conscience, so I'm willing to pay you monthly so that you can take care of of the baby, but after hearing this, we can't be together anymore because White's my mans and I can't continue to live like this knowing that I've destroyed his family by sleeping with his girl."

Even though Nasty wanted children, he knew that to become a father in a situation like this would only cause more problems for him.

Tina disregarded his last comment about them being together anymore. She didn't even look at him when she said, "It costs five hundred dollars. I ain't got time to be breeding any children right now because I got too many other things that I want to do this year."

Nasty was upset with her decision.

He snapped, "Well here! Take it then,"he said as he grabbed the money from his wallet. "I can't tell you what to do, all I was saying is that I don't approve of your choice."

Nasty handed her five hundred dollars. Tina reached for the money and put it in her purse without saying another word.

"When are you going to do it?"Nasty said, as he tried his best to stay cool. But as soon as he asked her he thought about how he wanted to take back his words but it was too late.

Tina says, "As soon as I can get away from White. But more than likely, it'll be Monday or Tuesday at the latest,"she rubbed her stomach with both of her hands. As nasty watched her, he felt strange listening to her talk about having his baby inside of her and then destroying it. There was no doubt that the child was his. Tina was very careful about how she did things with Nasty and White. She was caught between both of them. Initially, she was making Nasty strap up with a condom. But when White stopped handling his business in the bedroom. she decided to take a chance in the ring with Nasty with the gloves off. Once her and Nasty began sleeping with each other unprotected she began keeping notes about every encounter they had, just in case something went wrong.

Nasty thought about the fact that he could be having a child, but he immediately blocked out the thought because it was over with between him and Tina.

Tina got up and asked, "I guess this it huh?"

"I guess so,"he responded and rubbed her back.

Tina got up in her feelings and walked off never looking back.

NASTY DROPPED HIS head as he told the story to Fernando.

"How did you find out that you had the baby?" Fernando asked

"I told you that White was my partner. I do have eyes and ears. I kind of figured that Tina was coming to meet me so that she could break things off with me. But her way of doing it was different than I thought. Tina lied to me, and that was something that I had to deal with. And only I knew the truth and I couldn't tell a soul. And to be honest with you; I was just thankful to know that you were still alive."

Silence filled the air between the two of them. They both stood quietly.

Fernando was stunned after hearing that Nichole's revelations about everything were true. All of the doubt that had been inside his head began to turn into anxiety. Fernando didn't have time to prepare himself for what was coming next. He already had too much going on as it was. But at that moment, the reality of what had happened was slapping him square in the face.

Fernando and Nasty made their war back in the house. Nasty turned to Fernando and says, "If my story don't add up, we can take a DNA test."

"I think that would be the best thing to do," Fernando responded.

"I will be right back." Nasty said.

Nasty went to the bathroom and grabbed a DNA kit out of his medicine cabinet. He came back and produced a sealed plastic bag that contained two clear vials. He handed Fernando one of the tests so that he could swab the back of his throat. After Nasty did the same, he sealed the containers.

"How long will it take to get the results?"Fernando asked.

"By tomorrow."Nasty said,

"Finally, I get some answers."Fernando said.

Fernando's mind drifted off thinking about the next thing that he had to do, and that was to deal with Nichole, who was most likely his sister.

Fernando realized that his mom was going to have to answer some tough questions about what had happened in the past. But, he wasn't sure if he would ever get the chance to do so being that he was on the run. So, how was he going to see his mom? That was the million dollar question.

Monea came into the room and grabbed the samples from Nasty. He gave her instructions on where to take them. She nodded and then left to take the samples to get them tested.

Once she left the room and was out of sight, Fernando asked Nasty, "Were you ever married to anyone?"

Nasty shook his head from left to right and said, "Naw, I never married anyone physically but, I was married to the streets because that's all I knew."

"But she was married."Fernando asked sarcastically.

"I know it was wrong, but I was young, and so was she. Listen, we all do things when we are young and dumb that we ultimately regret later in life and I am sure Tina feels the same way."

Fernando felt warm so he unbuttoned a few buttons on his shirt. He thought to himself,

"Why am I so hot? Is the heat on? Or is it just me?"

Nasty continued to explain the situation to Fernando.

He said, "Look Fernando, your mother was lonely and felt betrayed. I have no idea what really happened between your mom and your dad, all I did was make her feel better for a while.

And that ended when she got pregnant with me, huh?" Fernando said sarcastically.

"I can see how you'd think that Fernando, but put yourself in your mother's shoes. Our relationship was a way for her to deal with the hurt that she was feeling with White. Was it right? Not at all. But it happened and you're the result of our love for each other at the time. So it wasn't all bad, because you're here,"Nasty explained.

Fernando just shrugged his shoulders and didn't say a word.

THE NEXT MORNING……

Nasty woke up and realized that he had to choose his words wisely and use caution from that point on. He knew that was the moment that he could either win Fernando's trust or run him away. Even though Fernando had doubts, he believed that Nasty was his father after the DNA results came back 99.9% positive.

Nasty knew that it was his fault that he hadn't been a part of Fernando's life. He didn't think that things would turn out this way between the two of them, however he also knew that Fernando's mother Tina was also to blame for him not being a part of his son's life. But Nasty didn't want him to question her just yet.

Nasty hadn't realized how nosey his girl Monea really was. He didn't know how careful he needed to be about speaking around her. However, everything was playing out just right and it didn't matter what she heard or said because by the time anything came out, Fernando would be in the hands of El Helzer. El Helza had found out that there was a strong possibility that the blood of Ricardo was on Fernando's hands and so because of that, there was a price to pay and the price was a life for a life.

Fernando had no clue that there was a price on his head and that he would soon be turned over to El Helza. He was focused on getting answers to his questions that continued to bother him.

# CHAPTER 17

## It's a first time for everything...

MOST FAMILIES WOULD be on the verge of breaking up during a time like this. The White family has strength, money, and a legacy to continue, but now they are in the middle of a crisis.

Grady Memorial Hospital was good at serving its patients during their time of trauma, and at a time like this, when there was suicide involved, it was critical for the nurses to handle the patient with care.

The RN rubbed Monique's back as she brushed past. Just a few days after the attempted suicide, Monique was still overwhelmed by what was happening with her brother being wanted and now with her mother in the hospital. it seemed as if situations went from bad to worse overnight.

Tina lay in the hospital bed sluggishly moaning. Upon hearing her mom, Monique rushed to her side and said, "Ma! I'm right here!"

Monique turned toward the door and yelled, "Nurse!"

The nurse advised Monique the medication that Tina had received had worn off.

Tina began talking and apologizing saying to Monique, "Please don't be mad at me Monique."Tina begins to cry. I was scared of losing another one of my men. Her cries became heavier. "I want my J.R. I want my son!"Monique embraced her and they cried together. "Mom, I'm going to run home, shower, and change. I'll be right back okay?"

Tina nodded and said, okay bring me back a few bagels with you please because I can't take another one of these hospital meals, everything they bring me tastes the same here and it's horrible.

"Okay ma, you know I got you. Give me about an hour at the most, but in the meantime try to get you some rest,"Monique said.

"Okay Monique, I love you,"Tina said.

"Love you too, ma,"Monique said and left.

THE HALLWAY OF the hospital was quiet, probably because the janitor had cut off the buffer. He had been eavesdropping ever since he heard someone scream out Jr. He wondered if it could be the same J.R. he knew. His curiosity was killing him and he decided to peek into room 170. Her visitor was gone and he thought to himself, "Good."

"Knock knock,"he said before entering. Tina rolled over and said, "Yes, may I help you?"She looked at the man's name tag and it said Calvin.

"I'm terribly sorry to bother you ma'am. I overheard you mention the name J.R. and I wanted to know if it is the same guy that goes by Fernando?"

Calvin knew that he had to be careful with the delivery of his questions.

Calvin continued, "If this is the same guy, he was dating my daughter for a while and she is always speaking nice things about him."He paused to let what he had just told Tina sink in.

"Yes sir, that's my son."

"if you don't mind me asking, how's the young fella doing these days?"

"Sir, if you don't mind, I'd like to keep your daughter and my son's business between the two of them. I don't mean to sound rude, but now is not the time for me to talk about or focus on anything else other than my health Mr. Calvin."

"Forgive me for my rudeness, let me make it up to you and grab you some lunch. How does that sound?"

"That's very thoughtful of you sir, but my daughter is bringing me something to snack on when she comes back."

"Snack on? Are you sure that's going to be enough? And I insist. Just name it and it is yours, pretty lady. "Well since you won't stop pulling my leg and trying to make me smile, I guess so because my daughter will be gone for at least an hour so just ummm…get me whatever you're eating. I won't be picky,"Tina said.

"Your wish is my command, young lady,"Calvin said, then turned rushing off leaving a smile on Tina's face.

GUILT RAN THROUGH Hollywood's body, and one thing that he wasn't good at doing was coping with feeling bad about something. All of this was weighing heavy on him. When things seemed to be too big or too heavy for Hollywood to carry, one thing that gave him strength to take on the world was Molly.

Before he and Fernando departed, Fernando made sure to keep his next destination concealed. Hollywood was his family now, but seriously who could be trusted at a time like this? Hollywood tried calling Fernando over and over again but could not reach him. He became agitated, "Where the fuck is this nigga at?"He pounded on the steering wheel in frustration. "You want to hide out like a little b****. I got some for that s***."He flicked on his blinkers. He glanced in the rear view mirror. "F***!"It was blue lights and he almost panicked until the police car swerved around him and hit the gas going after someone else. Hollywood hit a huge line after that scare. He drove with his knee on the steering wheel and hands-free so that he could make sure that he didn't drop any of the molly as he snorted it. That line of Molly went straight to the head. He shook off the head rush. Hollywood's eyes and mind were wide open. His emotions were all over the place. They were mixed with some good and a lot of bad. His thoughts went straight to thinking that his homeboy was intentionally ducking his calls.

MONIQUE STEPPED OUT of the shower feeling exhausted to the point that she didn't even dry off with a regular towel, she just allowed her body to air dry as she flopped down on the bed with her hair wet and all. She ran her index finger around her belly button and rubbed the beautiful life that was in her stomach. All she could think about was the tragic events that were suddenly surrounding her family. Her phone began vibrating and the doorbell rang at the same time. She looked at her phone and wrapped her hair with the towel and threw on and oversized t-shirt. As she approached the door, she was thinking to herself about the last time when she answered the door without seeing who was on the other side. This time, she was determined to take caution. She looked through the peephole and asked, "Who is it?"On the other side of the door Hollywood recognized the voice. "Monique. open the door, it's Hollywood!"She unlocked each latch and then opened the door. Monique pulled Hollywood inside of the home and said, "Where in the hell is my brother at Hollywood?! I seen the news the other day and I ain't trying to hear no b******* neither!"Hollywood yelled back, "Slow down Mo, slow down!"Then he sat down and wiped the sweat from his nose with his forearm and continued. "Honestly, I came here looking for bro my damn self because I ain't seen him since the other day."

Monique shot back, "N***** you better not be lying. The both of y'all stupid as hell anyways! What the f*** was y'all thinking?!"she said and punched him in the arm.

Monique's nipples were standing at attention due to her excitement and the breeze from the ceiling fan.

Hollywood said, If you keep punching on me, I might hit you back girl so stop!"

Monique ran up in his face and said, "I ain't scared! What! What you gone do?"You gone to do me like you did……

Hollywood cut her off just as she was trying to finish her sentence. He pulled her by the waist towards him and met her mouth with his tongue. To his surprise, she didn't resist and they began kissing. He was a bit aggressive. The more he roughed her up, the hotter she got. And before she knew it. her shirt was flown over her head and onto the sofa and he was on top of her. She undid his belt buckle and unzipped his pants, watching them hit the floor. She paused and looked down and noticed that he was big. Her p**** instantly started throbbing and dripping.

Monique said aggressively and seductively, "You want to bust up here like you want some s***, well let me see you come get this p****."she backed up to the sofa, laid down and spread her legs to let him see what he was in store for. Hollywood's tongue was the first to touch her body and say hello to her p**** lips. He was on his knees with her legs up under his arms hijacked in the air.

Monique moaned heavily, "Ooooooh ooooooh yeah…yes!"she screamed.

Hollywood inserted two of his fingers into her p**** and circle his tongue around her clit as she grinded her hips on his face.

"So I…can't… have that dick?"Monique exhaled.

To her, it felt like Hollywood was trying to eat her walls out, and she couldn't take it anymore; she wanted him inside of her. Hollywood pulled back and his goatee was shining and glistening from the wetness of her p****. She grabbed his dick and stroked his manhood and then guided him into her juice box. The length and size of Hollywood's dick made her think to herself that this is what it must feel like when a baby comes out of you. She was in ecstasy and Hollywood didn't waste any time putting her in a missionary position. He pounded on her for almost 30 minutes straight and without any second thought, he filled her inside with all of his cum.

Instantly, Monique flip the script and said, "Get your s*** and get out! That's all you want to do! Go! Get out Hollywood!"

And without a word, Hollywood complied. He pulled his pants up and left.

# CHAPTER 18

## The Final Destination

$10,000 IS A LOT OF money to just give to someone with no plans of them returning it to you without a profit. Most people would say that only fools think like that. 10 bands will put a dent in anyone's pocketbook or wallet, and as for Calvin, that was just the case. He had just put himself in a position to be in the palm of someone else's hands as far as his money was concerned. Calvin was in a situation that put his life on the line. Before he had a chance to confirm his old running mate, Alex was dead. Calvin said to himself if he ever had the chance he would definitely take full advantage of the situation and get his money back.

BY THE TIME CALVIN left Tina's room, he hoped that his seed had been planted. While he buffed the floor, he noticed Monique getting off the elevator. He wanted to approach her but had second thoughts about doing so because he knew that he had to come correct to a woman like her. She was the type of woman who needed security and only a man with money could provide that type of lifestyle. And at Calvin's age, he wasn't about to go back to the hood and start back hustling which could ultimately cause him to end up in prison, reading *The 48 Laws of The Chain Gang.*

MONIQUE OPENED THE door to her mother's room to see food everywhere. She was surprised. Monique says, Ma! I thought I told you to rest and not to walk around?"

"Child I haven't left this bed. This very nice gentlemen treated me to all of this,"Tina responded.

"Who's the gentleman?"Monique asked dryly.

Tina sensed Monique's uncertainty and said, "Nobody really, he looks as if he works here."

"Is he a doctor?"Monique asked curiously.

"Try a janitor girl,"Tina said.

Monique chuckled and said, "So, I guess you're good with this?"as she held up the bag.

"My old butt about to put on some pounds if they don't release me soon. Have you heard anything about my status or when they are going to release me,"Tina asked.

Monique hesitated and said, "No not yet Ma! But I'll check on it later, right now just focus on resting and healing."

It hurt Monique's heart to have to tell her mom a lie. She knew that the doctors had told her that her mom had to be treated at a mental hospital after she was released. She was also informed that if her mother didn't comply, the police would put her in custody. Monique didn't know how she was going to tell her mom that devastating news, and right now was not the appropriate time but eventually it would come.

Three days later.......

CALVIN WAS DETERMINED to get as much information as he could from Tina so every time one of her visitors would leave, Calvin would pop up and use his charm to get Tina to answer as many questions as he could about Monique.

Tina knew that if her daughter found out that a janitor had been asking questions about her, she would be infuriated and that was one thing she didn't need in her life right now because there were already enough bad things happening in her life as it is.

Tina began to feel more and more comfortable as her and Calvin talked. He knew he had to pour it on thick so that he could get her to reveal to him her son's whereabouts, but Tina didn't have a clue as to what was going on and the reason behind Calvin's visits. All she knew was that the janitor was being extremely nice to her. After trying to get Tina to tell him about her son's whereabouts, Calvin began to get discouraged and feel like it was too late for him to get his money back so he decided to go to plan b.

~~~

10:15pm

"MOM, I'M GOING to take it in for the night okay so I want you to get some rest. I'll be back first thing tomorrow to check on you okay?"Monique said.

Tina yarned and said, "Okay, love you baby, and drive safe."

Mom, don't worry about me, I'll be fine, you just get yourself some rest because you're going to need it okay."Monique responded.

"Yes ma'am mom,"Tina jokingly said and crawled under the covers.

"Girl bye" Monique said then she hit the lights and left the room.

The front of the hospital was flooded with homeless and sick people. Monique tried not to stare or look at them. She held her purse close and kept her eyes forward. Before she reached the parking garage, she stopped as she realized that she left her keys on the TV in her mom's hospital room. She turned around and headed back to the room. On her way back, all she kept hearing from the homeless people was, "Can you spare some change ma'am?"

Monique said no and walked even faster to get back to grab her keys.

TONIGHT, CALVIN WAS on a mission and he decided to wear a different uniform other than his usual brown Dickies suit. He also wore a pair of black leather gloves to help him with his mission.
~~~

He made it to Tina's room and opened her door. As the door opened, it squeaked just a little. Tina was sound asleep and her monitor beat steadily as Calvin approached her bedside. Calvin knew that if he used a gun or suffocated Tina, it would be two alarming. He needed to be as quiet as possible when he did the job and using a needle with a heavy sedative medication would do just the trick. He had plans to do the job and be in and out. Calvin tiptoed over to her IV cord and inserted the needle and just as he was about to squeeze the needle's fluid into her IV the door to the room came open.

"What the hell are you doing!"Monique shouted.

She ran back out of the door and screamed, "Help! Help! Help! Somebody help please!"

Calvin dropped everything as he felt like he was stuck between a rock and a hard place. He had to think quickly on his feet as he dashed out of the room and towards the emergency exit stairwell. Monique pointed towards the direction that he ran in, letting the security guards know where he was. The security guards radioed for backup while giving them the location of the suspect. Calvin ran as fast as he could down a flight of stairs skipping two or three of them at a time. By the time he reached the third floor, he was met by security and they were all over him.

"Freeze! Don't move! Get on the ground!"The security guard ordered.

Calvin didn't resist. He got on his knees on the ground.

"Fuck!"was all he could say right before he was roughed up and handcuffed.

MONIQUE WENT BACK into her mother's room that was now filled with doctors making sure that everything was okay.

Monique asked, "How is she doing? Is everything okay?"

"Ma'am, we're going to need you to step back outside for a moment while we run some more tests.""Thank you for understanding,"the nurse said and walked Monique back out of the door into the lobby and assured her that the doctors were doing all that they could to help her mom.

As Monique sat down in the lobby she said to herself, "Why did the nurse say to me they're doing all they can to help my mom?"

Then it dawned on her that there was a problem, Monique jumped up and rushed back to the room and this time there was no stopping her.

Monique burst into the room and yelled, "ma! ma! ma!"

The doctors looked around at Monique and said, "Ma'am, we need you to step back out of the room please."

Tina was laying on the floor and one of the doctors was doing CPR and another one held the EKG machine close by.

Monique yelled again, "Ma! Ma!"

Tina wasn't moving. She just laid there.

"Somebody please say something!"Monique cried out.

One of the doctors looked at her and said "Ma'am, I'm sorry but…"

FERNANDO WAS ENJOYING laying up in the West Coast sun. Everything that he wanted or needed was at his beck and call. Fernando didn't have to worry about anything, and that allowed him to have a peace of mind. Returning to Atlanta was not an option for him. He was content where he was.

He turned on his phone so that he could check out the Atlanta News. When he opened the news thread, the top story in the feed was about he and Hollywood's escapade. He thought maybe Nasty could help him. Fernando knew that Nasty was connected and plugged in to the who's who, so maybe just maybe he could make one of Fernando's problems go away.

Fernando rolled over on the bed away from the beautiful sun's rays that were entering the window. He jumped at the sight of Nichole standing there without him knowing it. She had been there in the room watching him scroll the news timeline on his phone.

"Whoa! What are you doing here?"he said surprisingly.

"You must have forgotten that this is my dad's house?"Nichole said as she sat down on the edge of the bed.

"Nichole, I'm talking about in this room!"Don't you think it's rude to be waking people up like this?"Fernando said.

"Boy please! Rude my butt! You wasn't sleep. You was on your phone," she said.

Nichole slid her hand under the cover and ran it up Fernando's leg.

He pushed her hand back and said, "Nichole you tripping! Shawty your memory must be bad. We're family!"

"Not me! I ain't your family boy!"She said seductively and moved closer to him.

Nichole continued, "You need to stop denying me and get with it. I ain't gone hurt you, I promise."

She grabbed his dick and Fernando tried to resist but he couldn't.

He said, "Nicole, I'm not about to fuck you girl!"

As Fernando reached for her hand, she squeezed his dick tighter.

Fernando gasped saying, "I…I…I…can't."

He sounded like he was stuttering.

"I don't want to fuck neither boy! I want to taste it!"She said.

Nichole flings the cover back, and puts her mouth on the bridge of his manhood.

As she slobbed on his dick going up and down giving him some of the best head he had ever had, Fernando was in ecstasy until the door burst open and they were shocked by masked gunmen storming in the room. The six masked men quickly grabbed Nichole. She screamed and kicked. They covered her mouth and carried her out of the door. The other masked men ordered for Fernando to stand up and come with them. At first, he thought it was the feds until he heard them speaking Spanish. Fernando was confused as to what was going on and he wondered where Nasty was during this raid. The masked men ordered Fernando down the stairs and out of the house into the tinted out black SUV. Fernando was nervous and he decided that it was best that he didn't say anything until he had the chance to think things through. And because everything was moving so fast, he didn't have time to prepare a defense but knew that he had to make his next move his best move. The ride seemed like it took forever. Fernando was watching everything, he looked at each one of the men and took mental notes about details that he could use to his advantage. He knew that he couldn't take his eyes off of the prize. He wanted to make sure that he didn't miss anything. And he didn't. Finally the SUV came to a stop. Instantly the doors flew open. The heat from the sun was scorching hot. Fernando was snatched from the truck and placed on his knees. He could feel every inch of the desert's cracked surface. Tiny dust storms formed in the distance. The blowing wind caused Fernando's vision to blur. He wiped his eyes with the sleeve of his shirt so that he could regain his visual focus. Once his vision became clear, he looked up and noticed Nasty standing next to a short curly haired Hispanic dressed in a white linen suit. The Hispanic had two gold chains that held Jesus pieces on them, and on his wrist he adorned a 18kt gold iced out Rolex. Between the two of them, you could tell who the boss was.

"Little White! I can see that you have grown from the little boy that I used to know."The Hispanic said speaking excellent English.

He nodded his head at the gunmen and they stood Fernando up on his feet.

"Who are you? And what's going on?"Fernando asked.

Nasty didn't say a word, he just stayed quiet. He knew that the less he said the sooner it would be over, and even though he didn't like the idea, he didn't feel like he had no other choice but this one.

The well dressed Hispanic walked up to Fernando and said, "My name is El Helza, but to you…Hell!"

He turned away and snapped his fingers twice. His assistant opened the door, El Helza and Nasty hopped back into the SUV and the driver pulled off. Anxiety filled Nasty's stomach about the thought of his son being left to die.

Once they got about one hundred yards away from the scene. What Nasty felt had him thinking that he had lost his mind. Without a second thought, he whipped out his gun and pointed at the dome of El Helza. The driver instantly slammed on the breaks. Before he could react three shots reached the back of his head. Nasty jumped out of the SUV and dragged each of the men out of the truck and threw them on the ground. He jumped back into the SUV and headed back to where he had just left Fernando.

TWO GUNMEN ESCORTED Fernando to his final destination. Just ahead of them was a cross sticking out of the dirt. When Fernando saw the shallow hole in the ground he shook his head in disbelief seeing that he was walking to his own grave.

One of the gunman spoken Spanish directing Fernando forward saying, "Andale, andale, punta!"

The hitman noticed that El Helzer's SUV had returned and was approaching at a high speed. The closer that it got, the man noticed that it wasn't slowing down so they became alarmed and concerned so they jumped out of the way. They didn't take any shots at the vehicle because they didn't know if El Helzer was inside.

Once the vehicle came to a halt and the doors flung open, the men were surprised when gunshots rang out towards them. They tried to run and escape, however the shots pierced through them as they fell to the ground. Fernando grabbed one of the AR-15s and began to unload the clip to the assault rifle. Once all of the men were dead, Fernando turned around and looked at Nasty with a look that could cut right through him. Fernando stood staring at Nasty for a while contemplating what he should do. Nasty also stood there staring at Fernando without his gun pointed at him. Fernando couldn't speak, however Nasty broke the silence by saying, "I just couldn't go through with it. I just couldn't. You're in my son!"

Nasty took a few steps forward, but then stopped when Fernando raised his weapon and said, "Stop! Don't come any closer. Throw me them keys. I'll take it from here!"

Nasty responded with grief at first saying, "Can't you see I came back for you?"

He continued trying to be demanding and said, "Now lower the gun son and let's go!"

Nasty took a few more steps forward but was ordered to stop again.

This is the last time I'll tell you to not come any closer. The next time, I ain't doing no talking, and miss me with that son s*** n*****. If you was thinking like that from jump street, we wouldn't be here in the first place. Now back the fuck up!"

Nasty started walking backwards.

"Go on, keep on walking nigga!"Fernando said with disdain in his voice.

Nasty kept moving backwards, and before he knew it, he had fallen back into the manhole that was dug for Fernando.

Nasty yelled upon falling down, "Awh!"

If you want to live, you better stay put until I pull off.. you hear me?"Fernando yelled.

"You can't leave me like.."Nasty screamed.

"Pow!"

Nasty jumped!

"I ain't gone miss the next time nigga!"Fernando said, backing up to the suburban.

Once he reached the driver's seat, he tossed the AR on the passenger side and pulled off. His blood was boiling in fiery heat as his heart pumped fast and sweat ran down his face. Fernando didn't know where he was going. He was just driving blindly not knowing which way to go. He had come too far and definitely knew that he was not going back to Georgia. After driving for a while, Fernando almost wrecked when he felt a steel barrel rest on the back of his head. He didn't even want to turn around so he just looked in the rearview mirror at his accomplice's face.

"You know that you would be dead right now if you would have pulled that trigger back there.""The voice said. She kept her aim focused as she moved to the front passenger seat. She threw the assault rifle on the back row.

"Nicole, how did you.. I thought..''Fernando nervously rambled.

"I was in the second truck. All you had to do was be patient,''She continued. "Now turn this baby around and go get my dad, or should I say our dad,''she said grinning.

That right there showed him that she had more screws loose than he gave her credit for. Fernando turned around. The wind had picked up, and so did the dust. It was hard to see ahead, but Nicole's eyes zeroed in on her dad through the debris. The suburban stopped. Sore and out of breath, nasty climbed in the back seat of the car. once he got in, he sat quietly for a second so that he could catch his breath.

"Dad, are you good?''Nicole asked.

She thought about helping him because it seemed like he needed it, but her attention had to remain on her brother Fernando because she wasn't sure what he would do.

"Babe, I'm good. Come, I'm glad everybody is here who's supposed to be here,''he said, breaking the ice between him and his son.

Fernando shot in a cold stair in the rear view mirror and said, "So, where in the hell are we going?"

"Home,''Nasty said.

"However, we have to make a quick stop because they will be coming for us."

"They?''I thought we passed El Helza's dead body back there?"

"Well son, we did. But guys like Hell come with a lot of extra soldiers than that. Believe me, I know because I used to work for him."

Nasty begin calculating the amount of time that they had to get away. He estimated 30 minutes at the most.

ONCE THEY REACHED Nasty's estate, Nasty was the first to jump out. Nichole was close behind him on his heals. Fernando thought desperately about pulling off.

He thought to himself, "Where would I go?"

Something drew his eyes to the back window of the vehicle. He saw the Humvees and two SUVs appear. They were obviously on a mission. Rifles hung out of all of the windows. Fernando knew he had to think quickly, so he slid out of the passenger side door in order to avoid a gunshot to the back of the head.

Fernando made it to the front door of the house. He busted through the front door yelling they're here they're here!

Nasty and Nicole were coming down the steps as he was shouting. Nichole ran to the windows and peeked out to see how many of them there were.

She said to Nasty, "Dad what are we going to do now?"

"We gone fight!"Nasty said.

He ran over to his wall unit and there was no time for him to use a key, so he used his foot to open it. Once it opened, Nasty tossed Fernando an AK-47. He looked at his daughter and said, "Babygirl stay low. Please."

She ran to the back of the house and took cover.

Fernando looked at his dad and said, "Let's do it!"

Just as they agreed to go to war, bullets exploded through the front door. Both men hit the floor and took cover. They crawled on the floor to get a better shot. Nasty peeped out of the curtains. He saw shooters everywhere and they were moving in fast. Nasty started shooting first and then Fernando followed suit, but the òps had the house surrounded.

Fernando yelled, "Imma hit the left wing to try and stabilize a few of them, so be on the lookout and keep your head up!"

"Okay, be careful!"Nasty said as he nodded acknowledging Fernando's plan.

They looked at each and didn't say a word. As soon as Fernando hit the corner, two gunmen were trying to climb through the window. Luckily, he saw them first. When the gunmen looked up it was too late. Fernando began spraying them with bullets. Once they fell to the ground, he ran over to them and kicked the weapons from their reach. He saw six armed men passing by the window and he ducked so that they couldn't see him. However, he noticed that they had kidnapped Nichole and he was shocked.

He thought to himself, "Damn! How did they get her?" He wanted to take a shot at the guys, but he didn't have a clear one so he forgoed the thought. Even though he wanted badly to give them the business, he wished that he knew where Nasty was so that they could come with another action plan.

NASTY GOT DOWN on one knee as if he was seeking cover. He placed his back against the suburban. He scanned the area. He looked to his left and then right and counted 12 shooters that were on the ground. He didn't know how many more there were in the vehicles. They were on high alert as they looked for him and Fernando. Nasty knew in his mind that he could only take down maybe two or three of them at best. He saw the rear door of the Humvee close as they shoved his daughter forcefully inside of it. She tried to resist but was overpowered. Once the door to the Humvee closed, its tires squealed on the pavement as the vehicle turned and sped off. All Nasty could do was watch in horror through the rearview mirror as his daughter's head was pushed down by the Hispanic assailant. Nasty watched helplessly as the Humvee made a right turn out of his estate with his daughter in tow. Nasty heard a single gun shot rang out from the front of his house. He looked up and saw Fernando clutching his stomach as he came out the front door. Nasty jumped up from behind the vehicle and ran towards Fernando yelling, "Son are you okay? Talk to me son. Talk to me"

Fernando fell to his knees and said, "They got her."

"I know, but let me get you wrapped up first. That wound looks pretty bad."

Nasty helped his son up and said, "Take it easy, We'll get her back. I promise you that!"

Nasty tried his best to conceal how much he was hurt because of them taking his daughter.

They walked back inside of the house and Nasty told Fernando to lay down on the floor so that he could clean up the wound that grazed his hip.

Fernando said softly, "We can't do this by ourselves, we're going to need some additional help and I got the perfect man for the job. But first I think we need to get out of here."

Nasty agreed. He patched up Fernando and helped him outside to the Suburban.

Nasty jumped in the driver's seat and said, "We've got maybe 24 hours before they kill her. Nichole is the bait and I'm the fish because they know that I'm coming to get her, so we ain't playing by no rules."

He pulled off from the driveway and continued, this is gangland out here and these cartel acts are not similar to the dudes back in the city, so please don't send for no Ricky to come out here and handle a job like this because I need a guy who is willing to kick down doors and shoot the shit out of who's ever on the other side of it,"Nasty said to Fernando and then handed him the phone.

Nasty you got to trust me on this. And hopefully they're just holding her, waiting for you. "They're going to torture her!"Nasty growled.

"You sound like I want something to happen to her. You need to…." Fernando said.

"Don't tell me what I need to do!"Nasty screamed.

"This ain't going to work if you don't calm down and remember I didn't ask for none of this."

"You're right, but my daughter is all I got!" Nasty said.

He looked his son in his eyes and said, " And you."

Fernando knew from that point on, he had to either get with it or head back to Atlanta. And all Georgia had to offer for him was a prison sentence.

# CHAPTER 19

## The last dance

HOLLYWOOD'S LAST SEXUAL encounter with Monique was epic in his book. She was sexy, cool, and she had money. She was a total package. But between his occupation and her family's last name, that wasn't enough to end any future plans thinking of togetherness with her. Hollywood was good with just the fuck session he had with Monique. And while thinking about their last rendezvous, his phone began to ring. He thought it was a coincidence that It was Fernando calling. He answered the phone, happy to hear Fernando's voice. He was glad to know that his fam was good. Fernando asked Hollywood to come to the West Coast and Hollywood gladly accepted Fernando's invite. Hollywood was also feeling like his time was running short in Atlanta, and he was tired of ducking and dodging the cops everyday. Hollywood was more than ready to get in the air on a flight to the West Coast. It was a good thing that Nasty had a friend who worked at The Hartsfield International Airport. They owed him a favor and he was ready to cash in on it. Nasty's friend was able to hook him up with a ride on a jet, and he enjoyed every minute of the first class service that he received. Flying in a jet was a first time experience for Hollywood. The five hour flight was intriguing, and by the time he touched down in Los Angeles, Hollywood had seen more than he had ever seen before and knew that from that point on, living in Atlanta solely was about to be a thing of the past. When Hollywood exited the plane, he was greeted by Fernando and Nasty. Once the salutations were completed, the driver opened the doors to the luxury sedan and they all jumped inside. Hollywood's main focus on getting straight to the business at hand so he forgoed sightseeing.

WHEN THE MAN on the other end of the phone informed Nasty about the tunnels that were beneath the mountains on the outskirts of Sherman Oaks, he took the information and used the YG. Nasty knew the area, and he didn't expect them to possibly be hiding out where the drugs were being stashed.

There was one guard standing outside of the entrance. The distance from where they were spying on the location was at least 200 yards away.

Fernando asked, "What else do you see Hollywood?"

"I don't see a major problem so far. It's just one person on post, but ain't no telling how many there are on the inside,"Hollywood said.

"Let me take a look,"Nasty said as he grabbed the scope. He saw the door open. Monea walked out and nasty said surprised, "What the f***?"he was in shock. He stood up and dropped the scope. "What's going on? What do you see?" Fernando asked and picked up scope. Fernando's eyes followed Monae to the Jeep. "She ain't supposed to be here. Why is she here?"Fernando asked Nasty as he looked with concern.

"That bitch must have been f****** with the boss the whole time?" Nasty said angrily.

Hollywood was lost and didn't know what they were talking about. He didn't care because all he wanted to do was handle the business at hand.

He said to himself, "These n.... talk too much."

Hollywood got frustrated with them and said, "F*** all that talking let's go shoot this s*** up. All this talking ain't going to get Shawty back. Wazaam!"

Nasty nodded in agreement because he knew Hollywood was right. The longer they stood there talking, nothing would get done and he wouldn't get his daughter back. So they had to do something. Fernando flung the shoulder strap or the AK-47 across his chest and checked to see if the safety was off.

Hollywood and Fernando did the same. They stayed low and moved in closer. The three of them moved over the hills and into the bright afternoon sun making their way towards the target. The location was remote and quiet. It only had a small narrow road with only one way in and one way out. The location was definitely secure.

"Do y'all hear that?"Fernando stopped and asked.

"Yeah, it sounds like whatever it is, it's got a diesel motor in it,"Nasty said.

Hollywood jumped out onto the narrow road with his AK-47 pointed at the vehicle, ready to fire.

Fernando and Nasty stood by frozen for a second then they raised their weapons as well. The driver of the Jeep didn't see the ambush coming and the person driving the vehicle slammed on brakes. They were surprised to see that it was Monea and she was by herself.

NICHOLE LAID ON the floor covered with dirt and tried not to move. they had stripped her down so that she was wearing only her bra and panties. A plastic bag with only a few holes in it was tied around her head. Even though she desperately needed to go use the bathroom, she wasn't about to ask her captors to do so. They had already kicked her repeatedly for attempting to sit up straight. The two men who had been watching her didn't have any empathy or did not bother to say one word. They just put their boots to her ribs and kicked her repeatedly. Nichole did her best to survey her surroundings. She was almost certain that they had her somewhere underground. The floor was not paved, just dirt and even the filthy bag on her head had a dirty texture to it. She heard them speaking Spanish over the walkie talkies, which caused the men to start moving around the room. Nichole started wondering what was happening. All of the sudden, one of the men came and picked her up and threw her over his shoulders. She could feel that they were walking down several flights of stairs to get to where they were going. Every time the man touched a step, he would turn around and her head would brush up against the wall. She heard a door open which sounded like it was old because of how it squeaked. Once they brought her inside of the door, they dropped her on the floor like she was a sack of potatoes. Nichole rolled on her side and attempted to sit up. One of the men kicked her and flipped her onto her back. Nichole coughed and moaned in excruciating pain. She began to seriously question who these men were and what kind of people would treat her like this. Nichole heard the two men mumbling and talking in a distorted tone and immediately they rushed out of the room. Seconds later, the old wooden door squeaked as it opened with a bang and Nichole had a horrible feeling in the pit of her stomach that it was all over for her.

NASTY OPENED THE door to the dark stonewalled room. He walked across the dirt floor towards Nichole and looked down at her naked body as she lay there trembling with fear. He bent down and pulled the plastic bag off of her head. She looked up at him in shock as she blinked her eyes to try and regain her vision. He took off his shirt and reach down and covered her with it around her waist before the other man came downstairs and saw her that way.

When they heard movement coming towards them, Nichole clutched the shirt and tried covering her whole body. "Dad, I'm scared. I want to get out of here."

Nasty looked over his shoulder at the others and asked, "Is everything clear up there?"

"As clear as we gone get for now,"Hollywood said, reaching down and grabbing Nichole by the arm to help her off the floor.

The upper deck had bodies all over the floor and gunsmoke filled the air. They all moved with urgency as they exited the building.

Hollywood's next move was Monea. Hollywood knew she was a snake that had to have her head cut off.

Nasty wanted to know how long and why she did what she did. Sad to say, he wouldn't get a chance to even hear her sexy accent that he fell in love with anymore.

Hollywood walked up to the Jeep and added two nickel-sized holes into her forehead.

Nichole jumped as the gunshots rang out.

Hollywood's actions took everybody by surprise except for himself because he knew that too much baggage would only cause more problems. He unhooked Monea's wrist from the cuffs and her lifeless body hit the ground with a thump. They pulled off, leaving her in the dust.

THE HELICOPTER RIDE from North Carolina to the southern border took just 3 hours. Shortly after the helicopter landed, Fernando looked out of the window and got a gut wrenching feeling in the pit of his stomach. In addition to them being briefed on what was about to take place, there was an additional vehicle waiting on the runway that wasn't expected. Nasty looked at his daughter, Fernando, and Hollywood who all had the same look on their faces as well. He said, "Stay here and let me check to see if everything is still good as we planned."

FERNANDO GLANCED AT his father as he approached the unmarked cars outside. There were a total of four armed men. They were standing outside of their vehicles. Once Nasty reached one of the men, he handed him a cell phone. After a few minutes of conversation, Nasty returned to the chopper.

"It's time. Everything is all good so you can leave all the weapons here because beyond this point we are safe," Nasty said.

He nodded at the pilot giving him an all good signal. The landing strip was privately owned and so was the security. The security guards were put in place from a higher power much more powerful than El Helza. Everything was being handled by a different boss and in Mexico, they called him El Jefe. Which meant the "boss of all bosses" He was tied in with the politicians and the government in Mexico. In many people's eyes, El Jefe was the president. You couldn't stop him, so the best thing for the people to do was to step aside and let him continue feeding the people. He didn't discriminate against race or gender. Women around him knew their place and stood behind the man. Previous experiences left quite a few women scoring then dead after trying to step across the line that he had drawn. El Jefe was not pleased about how everything had gone down with El Helza, but the money was good enough to make just about anybody turn the other cheek. And El Jefe did so for the $1 million that was handed to him. Nichole glanced nervously out of the window as they drove. She said as calmly as she could, "Dad, I'm afraid that everyone in your line of work is aware of everything. And that's too risky."I don't think trusting these Mexicans is a……

She paused when the Hispanic in the passenger seat turned around and looked at her. These men you work for don't seem like at the end of the day we're going to turn out on top she whispering in her dad's ear. Why can't we ditch these guys?

Nasty lowered his voice to almost a whisper and said, "I know it seems raggedy, but as soon as we cross the border, I have a surprise waiting for everybody."The way her dad spoke clearly and with confidence gave her a sense of comfort. It also made her think about how she operated and came up with most of the things that she did which was with no remorse.

Nichole thought to herself and wondered if the surprise was meant for her, too. She said to herself, "A surprise for everybody?"

It was a quiet ride for everybody. 30 minutes later, they were approaching the checkpoint to Mexico. The border patrol became visible. There wasn't a car, truck, or motorcade in sight. It was only military personnel. And based on the driver's experiences, it made him and the front passenger feel uneasy about what was ahead of them.

Before the driver could react and hit reverse, the army of men had already begun approaching them with their weapons drawn and demanding for them to cut off the vehicles and show them their hands.

The military men yelled, "Show me your hands and cut off the vehicle!"

The driver looked over his shoulder at Nasty and said in his broken English, "I only follow orders from El Jefe, I don't know why?"

"I know,"Nasty said and pulled out his 9 mm and shot both men in the back of the head. Blood's better off over everybody. The next shot that rang out took everyone in the car by surprise. Hollywood and Nichole couldn't believe their eyes. Moments later the rear doors were snatched open and guns were pointed at everyone. Nasty extended his arms out and dropped his weapon not wanting to get shot. He wanted to let everything play out just how he knew it was about to......

To be continued.........

Coming Soon!!
Part 2

Black Hollywood
My Savages

# CHAPTER I

## The end always starts a new beginning...

One year later....

ONCE EVERYONE WAS seated, El Jefe stood up and cleared his throat so that he could get the attention of the room. Everyone in the room stopped what they were doing to hear what he had to say. El Jefe had everyone's undivided attention because this was the year's end meeting where bonus checks, promotions, and terminations took place. One particular person sitting at the table named Chico seemed to notice that there was something awkward going on. He and his mother caught eyes and exchanged a look of curiosity and then she turned her focus back to El Jefe.

"First of all, I want to tell everybody that me and my wife are very pleased that all of you showed up tonight,"El Jefe said and nodded with gratitude to everyone at the table. He continued saying, "And as I do at the end of each year, I would like to take this moment to give all of us a moment to slow down from the crazy fast pace that we have set for ourselves. I would also like to take this moment to thank all of you for all of your hard work and dedication towards what we have built here as a family. La Familia for life!"

Chico looked around at everyone at the table with disdain after hearing the word La Familia.

"I'm proud of all of you," His father said and purposely glanced in his son Chico's direction.

"Damn dad!" Chico exclaimed with a mischievous grin forming with his lips.

"Dad, you must be trying to break us down and make us all emotional or something. You sound like you are about to reveal to us that you're dying!" Chico said.

"Sorry mom,"he said, speaking in Spanish. Rather than adding gasoline to the fire, El Jefe said, "Let him be mi amor." Everyone was paying full attention now. With a glance at his wife, he whispered, "Mi amor, please don't be alarmed, but I will be ending our dealings in the business operations." The room went silent until his daughter Caroline stood up.

She exclaimed, "Why daddy? Did anything happen?"

"No princess. Nothing happened other than our age and you know we're getting older." He said and smiled.

"All of you were well informed about what's going on, and I want all of you to know that you can't do this line of work forever." He continued

"We've already lost three people, and we don't need to lose anymore. So we wanted to give you all of the time to adjust to the changes ahead.

Chico blurted out with disappointment in his voice, "Retiring…why are we talking about retiring!" His father noticed that his oldest son was caught more off guard than anyone. He looked hurt, and disappointed. "So if you're stepping down, then who's going to be in charge?" Chico asked seeking clarity. Although he was the oldest and possessed unquestionable loyalty to the family, nothing he did showed leadership. The room fell silent again; they all waited for an answer.

"I'm glad that question was raised son, I thought long and hard on this." El Jefe looked at each one of them with a deep and thoughtful look. He continued saying, "First of all, technically nothing's changed, I still run the borders and I am still going to hold majority of the shareholders, but in my absence, someone has to make decisions, and I have decided that the best person suited for the job is Señor Red." All eyes landed on Nasty, as everyone studied his reaction. El Jefe and no one else had any idea of what the future would bring. This was El Jefe's main reason for stepping down, so that he could prepare for what was to come.

~~~

ALL EYES WERE focused on Nasty the second his name fell from El Jefe's mouth. Nasty scanned the room, looking at his immediate family's faces, as he tried his best to not crack a smile. He was being chosen to lead the team and he was sure that there would be some resistance, but the decision was already made,.so he had to step up.

Chico didn't stand a chance at the role, and although Caroline was smart and the boss' man's daughter, she was a female and everybody knew how El Jefe operates. In his mind the men led and the woman followed. Then there was Hollywood who loved his title as the shooter and the family knew it.

Nicole on the other hand always showed up on the strength of her father and nothing more. Because she had been away for so long it took her a while to finally come out of her shell, and start leaving the house. She tapped in with the Mexicans' as well as with some of the ballers. Besides that Nasty felt he'd been working his ass off for this business long before they're ordeal so why wouldn't the boss man appoint him as a new leader? Nasty hadn't gotten a chance for everything to settle in his mind good before Chico stood up with his sister right on his heels pointing and shouting. Chico's attitude killed Nasty's moment immediately.

"Dad, why him? Why is Señor Red over me?"

Caroline jumped in. "Yeah Dad he's not even family!"

Jefe turned and looked in their direction and said,

"You want to know why? Because I said so, that's why?"

Caroline's spoiled nature gave her some leeway in most situations but the look in her dad's eyes was all that was needed to remind her to sit down. It was obvious that Chico wanted to say more but he held his tongue. Caroline foolishly mumbles something to get her brother and their father to look even more pissed.

"What was that?" he snapped. His eyes shifted back and forth from Chico and Caroline. "You two got something to say?"

Chico slumped down in his chair.
~~~

Caroline boldly stood up again and said, "I'm sorry Dad but I gotta say this, what about Santos and Carlos? How are you going to put Senor Red in charge and bypass them?"

The silence was oppressive and all eyes laid on the boss. Chico sat up, wishing he would have followed up with that question. Santos was Effie's younger brother who had been home from prison for only one year after serving 5 years for murder. If there was any questions of the level of power that their family actually possessed after Santos' trial, the ending results told the whole story. Santos kept it solid throughout trial even though the homicide committed was over an unpaid debt to the family business

Then there's Carlos Santos's twin brother. He lives by the same code which was to plead the fifth and family first! Their actions spoke for themselves

El Jefe glanced and looked at his wife knowing that this had been the subject of many conversations between them. He had become worn out from the conversation at hand. He sighed then looked at each of them and said, " I've already spoken with Santos about this and he's 100% behind my decision. As you all know that he's got other things he's handling right now."

"Yeah. But, what happens when he comes back?" Chico said to himself as he watched his sister take her seat.

The look on everyone's faces at the table led Jefe to decide to discontinue the meeting. After giving his last regards he assured if a problem was too heavy he taught it that he would still have an ear to the streets. Nasty slipped his iPhone from his pocket when he felt it vibrate, it was a text.

The text read: Just got some fresh meat in. you were the first one that came to mind. you interested? he lifted his head from the phone then look from left to right to make sure no eyes were on his iPhone screen he glanced over at Hollywood who was guiding his daughter with Chico and Caroline right behind them to the door then reply to the text

"Damn right I'm interested but I'm in a meeting, I just got a promotion and have a lot to celebrate so give me like 2 hours and then I can slip away."

The return text read: "Congrats on everything! I'll have my associate set everything up for the exchange"

Nasty glanced over at the El Jefe. He was not as confident in himself at that point as he should have been.  Nasty used to dream big about how he wanted to be a boss and now his dreams had become a reality, and he was on his way up.

# Meet the Author

BENNIE THOMAS is from Atlanta Georgia's Zone 6. He is a father who enjoys working out and keeping himself in shape. He also loves to read and write captivating stories. Benny has always dreamed of becoming an successful author and businessman. As he strives to do so, he stays humble and keeps God first. Follow him on all social media platforms for more updates.

# Meet the Coauthor

ANTHONY CLARK resides in Atlanta Georgia. He highly values his spirituality, and his relationship with the most high God. He is an avid reader, successful business man, motivational speaker, mentor, partner in education, and most of all a loving father. He enjoys spending quality time with his family, and working on his next project that is purposed to inspire others.

**Here are more literary works from the publisher.**

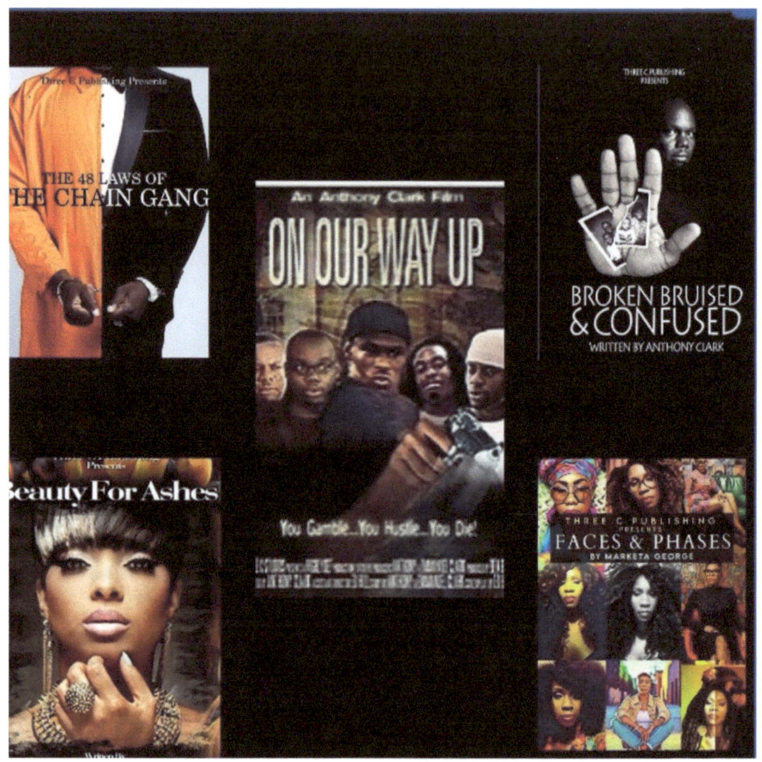


**Get your copy today online at:**
http://www.oldmp.com/brokenbruisedandconfused.htm
http://www.oldmp.com/48lawsofthechaingang.htm
http://www.oldmp.com/beautyforashes.htm
www.threecpublishing.com
www.Amazon.com
www.barnesandnobles.com